The Boy and the Eagle

TOM PUMA

Fulton Books
Meadville, PA

Published by Fulton Books 2024

ISBN 979-8-88982-550-0 (paperback)
ISBN 979-8-88982-551-7 (digital)

Dedicated to my grandson Silas

CONTENTS

C H A P T E R 1

The Test

July 16, 1945
Alamogordo, New Mexico
5:30 a.m.

The weather was poor, and clouds were moving into the area. There was word about canceling the test. All eyes were gazing through the windows of the bunker. The director of science for the Manhattan Project, Robert Oppenheimer, was peering through his window, sunglasses and pipe in place. All in the bunker were watching with great anticipation for what was about to take place for the first time in history: the first nuclear explosion that would ultimately end World War II.

As the countdown began—three, two, one—afar off was a sudden burst of light. It was unlike any light on earth because the heat of a nuclear explosion is unlike anything else on earth. They called its light cosmic. The temperature reached to the tens of millions of degrees. The heat was such that the air around it became luminous and incandescent. Then the air expanded outward, with an energy of the speed of sound, a blast that destroyed everything in its path.

Two hundred miles away in Amarillo, Texas, people could see the huge mushroom cloud forming, wondering what on earth just happened. In Silver City, New Mexico, windows shattered.

As the huge cloud expanded further into the atmosphere, a mother eagle sped across the sky toward a high mountain for shelter.

1

She caught the tail end of the fallout, trying to save herself and the baby eagles inside her. Her six-foot wing span moved her through the air with great speed. Earlier atop the Tularosa Basin, the mother eagle was scanning the area for food. Her keen sense of danger warned to leave the mountaintop when she spotted the bunkers, trucks, and tanks scattered in a circle down in the valley. The tail end of the cloud managed to engulf her as she caught a strong tail wind; she soared through the cloud and off toward Eagle Mountain off in the distance. Little did she know of the effects the fallout would have latter on for her baby eagles.

Exploring the Old Indian Caves

A bright light came beaming through the curtains of Silas Livingston's bedroom as he opened his eyes to greet the new day, rubbing his eyes as he sat up, pulled the covers off, and jumped out of bed. He bolted over to the window, looking at a beautiful sunrise just coming up over Eagle Mountain about two miles away. It was the beginning of the summer break from school, and Silas planned to make the best of it this year. The sunlight made his dirty blonde hair glow and his eyes sparkle. He opened the window to hear the sounds of farm life greet his ears. The chickens rustled about, clucking all over the place. The rooster gave his morning wake-up call like clockwork. The one old cow mooed out in the barn, waiting to be milked before she burst, and there was the rustling about in the kitchen. Mrs. Livingston was busy making pancakes and eggs, and the smell of her cooking almost lifted Silas off his feet as he got himself dressed and flew down the hallway and hopped into his chair.

"Well! Look who is up early this morning? That's a first," said his mom.

"It's the first day of summer vacation, Mom, and I don't want to waste it," replied Silas.

"And what are your plans, my young Tom Sawyer?"

"I think I will go to the old Indian caves over at Eagle Mountain to explore. I saw a beautiful eagle flying over there last week from the school bus."

"Well, okay, Silas, but you be careful. There have been wild dogs seen in that area the past few weeks. In addition, I wouldn't get to close to those eagles. They can be very dangerous," said Mrs. Livingston.

"I will be careful, Mom."

"But before you go anywhere, young man, there are your chores to be done first, like getting out to that barn and milking Lucy before she explodes and feeding the chickens and pigs."

As he finished his breakfast and flew out the door, he answered, "I'll get right on it, Mom."

Once he got outside, he stopped at the edge of the steps on the front porch to gaze upon the beautiful blue sky and Eagle Mountain off in the distance. It was as if it was painted on a huge canvas by the hand of God.

Mrs. Livingston could see Silas going into the barn as she washed dishes by the kitchen window. She was widowed for about two years and had the job of mother and father to him. Everyone in the town knew the family. They were always at church service each Sunday, and many of the townspeople would compliment her on the job she was doing, raising the boy and working a farm at the same time. She knew that Silas was familiar with the territory, so there was no problem with him getting lost. However, she did worry about his adventurous explorations around that mountain.

From the kitchen window, Mrs. Livingston could see the same beautiful sunrise as Silas did. She watched as he headed into the barn, picking up stones and throwing them out into the open field, causing some rabbits to scamper off and down into their holes. The barn doors were big and bulky. It took some elbow grease to pull them open, giving off a haunting sound from the rusted hinges. Once inside the dark building, Silas could hear Lucy further down in one of the stalls, mooing away. She knew Silas was in the building, and she wanted to be milked.

The barn had been built sometime around the 1860s, and it looked it: the long aisle down the center with old stalls of hay and old wood rails. The high loft stacked with hay and feed was a great place to play. Up in the loft was another door with a block and tackle for lifting heavy bundles up for stacking. Also a small hatch lifted up for roof access. Silas would go up on the roof at night to look at the moon and stars, and on clear nights, he would see shooting stars fly past him, heading off to Eagle Mountain and disappearing into the darkness. He now walked up to Lucy who had her head sticking out into the aisle, waiting for her milkman. Silas rubbed her head and ears, soothing her down.

"I'm here, girl. Let's empty you out. You must be bursting down there, and I would love a glass of fresh warm milk."

Silas grabbed the milk bucket and worked his way alongside Lucy and sat down on the tiny milking stool and began squeezing out some fresh milk into the bucket.

In the distance, he could hear the rooster giving his morning wake-up call again, thinking to himself, *I'm already up, Mr. Rooster.*

In minutes, the bucket was filled.

"There you are, girl, better now! I need to get this milk into the icebox, and you must be hungry."

Silas worked his way out from the side of the stall and out into the aisle, placing the bucket off to the side and grabbing a handful of hay, putting some into Lucy's feeding bin.

"There you go, girl. Eat up now. You don't want to get skinny, do you?"

Silas gave Lucy a last rub on her head and then turned, picked up the milk bucket, and carried it off to be poured into smaller milk bottles and placed in the icebox.

As he entered the kitchen, his mother already had the bottles on the kitchen table, waiting to be filled. This was a two-man job. One had to hold the funnel, and the other poured the milk into the bottles. Silas went and got himself two glasses from the cupboard and immediately poured some milk for his mother and himself. The two of them gave a toast.

"To the farm life," said Mrs. Livingston.

Then drinking down the milk in one gulp, they started their morning chore. They had this down to a science. Each knew what to do without saying a word to each other.

After about thirty minutes or so, the milk was all stored away. Now Silas was itching to go exploring. It was a long way to the old Indian caves at Eagle Mountain. She knew that Silas was well acquainted with the area. He knew every road and path around that mountain. Many of the old Indian caves had not been completely explored yet, and that was what worried her. She did not want him getting lost out there all alone. Silas was very careful not to go to deep into those caves anyway, at least, not without having someone else with him.

There had been stories about gold hidden in one of those caves by an old prospector. It was during the 1890s. While heading back into town to place his gold in the bank, Indians started chasing him. He headed to Eagle Mountain to hide. While carrying his gold on his back through the rough paths, he stumbled on one of the old caves and hid there for two weeks before he finally came out. However, not before he hid his gold in one of the caves, fearing the Indians might still be around. He figured that he would go back in the future to retrieve it. However, a week after he got back into town, they found him in his room dead from a heart attack. But the night before he died, he told his landlady about the gold hidden in the old Indian caves. Her husband tried looking for years to find it, but he died too. The story eventually turned to legend, and people just forgot about it. Silas knew about the legend too, but he never thought about looking for it. He figured if someone finds it, they will probably stumble over it when they were not looking for it. Although! It would help his mother and him with working the farm. There were many expenses.

"So, Tom Sawyer, what's the plan for today?" asked Mrs. Livingston.

"I'm off to Eagle Mountain, Mom."

"Well, I don't want you to be there too long. There are afternoon chores to be done, you know, so you be home before noon. Understand!"

"Sure thing, Mom. Home at noon. Got it," replied Silas. Then, kissing his mom on her cheek, he turned and bolted out the door, grabbing his bicycle on the porch and dashing down the three steps, and off he rode, Eagle Mountain straight ahead of him in the distance. There was a small cloud hanging over the top of its peak, giving a strange shadow of grays and blues. Silas had a chill run up his back as he gazed at the mountain.

The road to Eagle Mountain led him through a thick forest of tall pines. The people who first settled in the area made the path through the forest long ago. Riding in the forest was an adventure in itself: the sounds of wildlife all around him; birds chirping away in the trees; squirrels running everywhere, looking for nuts and pinecones; and rabbits sitting along the side of the road, then running off as he rode by. A stream that ran through the forest supplied much of the water in town. Silas could hear the sound of running water over the rocks as he came up to an old bridge that crossed over the stream and led out to the open field toward Eagle Mountain.

His heart beat faster as the mountain came closer and closer. Glancing halfway up, Silas could see, soaring with six-foot outstretched wings, a beautiful eagle gliding on a stream of air in majestic glory. What a remarkable sight. He stopped his bike to take in this picture of nature in its entire wonderful splendor. Feeling like a superhero, he put his foot to the pedal and raced off, leaving a cloud of dust behind him.

Soon he reached the base of the mountain. He could only ride his bike part of the way up the trails. The rest of the way, he would have to hike. Looking up, he could still see the eagle flying overhead. It was very high. *What a feeling*, he thought to himself, *to fly like that, soaring above the clouds and looking down on all the farms and the town, like the Lord looking down on the children of Israel from Mount Sinai.* The roughed terrain of Eagle Mountain was a challenge for even the best of climbers. Like Moses climbing up to get the Ten Commandments, Silas started up the narrow paths, stepping over sharp cactus and working his way through thickets and climbing over huge stones that seemed to be placed there by giants to prevent anyone from reaching the top of the mountain.

What was up there? he thought to himself.

He was ascending higher and higher; looking down, he could see his bicycle looking like a speck on the moon. Suddenly, a noise caught Silas's attention, moving in a bush nearby. He stopped dead in his tracks, gazing at the bush. He didn't move a muscle. The noise was getting closer and closer. Silas prayed it wasn't a rattlesnake. He had never climbed this high up. No one had ever climbed this high up on Eagle Mountain because of the superstition surrounding it about Indian spirits watching over it.

Mrs. Livingston was on the front sweeping the morning dust. While gazing at the mountain off in the distance, she stopped sweeping; and staring at the mountain, a sudden chill caught her while thinking about her son. Holding on to the broom with both hands, she bowed her head and prayed. "Lord Jesus, watch over my boy this day as he explores as boys do. Send your angles of protection to his side to guard him, in Jesus's name, amen." As she finished her prayer, the chill left her. She sensed a feeling of peace now and continued her sweeping. It was a short prayer, but her faith in God was unwavering. She found herself praying often for Silas ever since the death of her husband, and she always tried to teach Silas biblical values. A cool breeze blew past her face, and she stopped once again, her eyes closed, and inhaled as the breeze went by. Her light dress was blowing as she held on to the broom, as if the Lord was telling her "all is well."

Silas gazed at the bush, watching to see what would appear. It was then that a hand touched him on his shoulder. He spun around with a yell, eyes staring in fright and mouth wide open. Before him stood an old Indian. His features were as one of the Old West. His face was weathered by the sands of time. He had three huge eagle feathers tied to his headband hanging down along the side of his head. His clothes matched those of pictures Silas once saw in the towns Old West museum. In his right hand, he held long bow, and in his left hand, he held an arrow with beautiful eagle feathers, the bow always touching the ground. Silas didn't say anything; he just looked into the old Indian's eyes, and he soon felt a peace come over him. There was no fear in this place. The old Indian reached down to grab hold of Silas's hand and helped him up.

"I can see that you are on a mission, my boy. What do you seek on this mountain, one that climbs like a mountain goat?"

"I want to climb as high as the eagles and fly with them. I love to watch them as they fly above the clouds and mountaintops," replied Silas.

The old Indian looked to an eagle flying overhead, and pointing his arrow toward the eagle, he answered, "And so you shall, Silas, so you shall. But remember, little eagle, to whom much is given, much is required. There will be great responsibility."

"But where did you come from? How did you get up here and find me?" said Silas.

"I was sent here to guide you by request. You will fly with the eagles, and you will learn much wisdom, little eagle. You are on the right path. As long as you stay on the right path and listen to your heart, you will not stray. Now go, little eagle, what you seek is just ahead."

Silas turned his head upward toward a small ledge about fifty feet away. "But how did you know my name?" He turned back only to see that the old Indian was gone. Then spying the quest before him, he started up the steep slope toward the ledge, pulling himself over rocks and through bushes, always keeping his eyes on the ledge before him. Another few feet up and over the ledge, Silas pulled himself up and on to the ledge. There before his eyes lay a huge eagle's nest with three large eggs. Next to the nest lay the mother eagle, dead.

Off in the distance, Silas could see the whole town. It was like looking at his train set with all the small buildings and roads. And just beyond the horizon of the town off to the east were some big rain clouds. Silas's dad had taught him to read the clouds and knew when it was going to be a gentle rain or a storm, and this looked like a big storm coming, with huge black clouds of lighting. Looking at the surrounding rocks and cliffs above the nest, Silas knew that this nest would never survive when the rain came rushing down this slope. It would be washed down the mountainside. This is why many eagles don't survive.

He knew that he had to get down the mountain quickly now. "I can't take all these eggs down this mountain without breaking them all. I'll have to choose one and hope it survives," Silas said to himself.

So, choosing the largest egg, he scooped it up and wrapped it in his shirt pocket with the zipper. Then, looking up to heaven, Silas prayed, "Dear Lord, let this little bird live to fly above the mountains. Amen."

Then he started down the mountain as fast and as safe as he could before the storm hit. His legs carried him over rocks and cliffs. At times, he found himself sliding down slopes, scraping his thigh and hands. But his only thought was to save this egg. He soon found himself at the base of the mountain and by his bike. Hopping on, he paused long enough to reach into his pocket to check the egg. Thank God, it was still in one piece. Off he sped like the wind toward home.

Up on the ledge, gazing down and watching as Silas rode off, stood the old Indian. As he watched Silas going, his countenance then changed, a smile on his face.

CHAPTER 3

Hatching the Egg

As the first rays of the sun came up over the mountain, one beam shone through a tiny hole in the curtains of Silas's bedroom, like a magnifying glass pinpointing that light into his eyes. As he opened his eyes, rubbing and yawning, that old rooster gave his morning wake-up call. Leaping from his bed, Silas ran to the window. The first thing he saw was the chicken house.

The egg, he thought to himself.

Upon arriving home last night, Silas hid the egg in the only place he thought it would be safe. And what better place to put an egg but with other eggs. Silas dressed in a flash. The excitement was too great. He put on his shoes and started down the hall, through the kitchen, and out the door toward the chicken house. It was a pretty large chicken house, not the usual chicken coop people were used to seeing. A person could stand up in this one. Silas felt like an expectant father as he approached the door and entered. Goose bumps went through his body. Closer and closer, he came to where the egg lay, still warm in its new home. Silas just gazed at the egg, stretching out his hand to touch it. The light bulb above the egg gave off just enough heat to keep it warm. Silas didn't know what would happen.

From within the house called Mrs. Livingston, "Silas, come and eat your breakfast. It's getting cold. You can tend to your chores afterward."

Silas, kneeling by the egg and looking up to heaven, prayed, "Dear Heavenly Lord, please let this bird live. I don't know if it was right or wrong to take it from the nest. I was only afraid that it would get washed away in the storm. I promise to look after it and raise it up the best I can so it can return to the mountain where it belongs. Amen."

Turning to the door, he called out, "Coming, Mom, be right there."

A week had gone by; Silas was out in the garden, hoeing the tomatoes and cucumbers. Mrs. Livingston was cleaning the house. The dog, a small Australian collie, was lying in the chicken house just below the eagle's egg. All was pretty quiet on the farm that day.

Then! There was a tiny noise. The dog's ears went up. Then another noise, the dog's head went up, wondering where the noise came from. Suddenly, there was a large crack, and the dog started barking and barking. Silas's ears perked up, and looking toward the chicken house, he heard the dog barking away. *That's Pete.* "Mom, it's Pete barking over in the chicken house."

Mrs. Livingston came running out of the house. "What is it, Silas?"

The two of them ran into the chicken house to see Pete barking next to the eagle's egg. As they both came nearer, there was another crack. They stopped and stared at the egg. There were cracks all over the egg now. And it started moving. Mrs. Livingston held on to her son. "Silas, where did that huge egg come from? That is not a chicken egg."

"It's an eagle's egg, Mom. I brought it down from the mountain last week when I went exploring. The storm last week would have washed it down the mountain. It would never have survived. I am going to hatch it and raise it, Mom."

"What on earth could you do with an eagle, Silas? Do you know how big and dangerous they are? *No*, you cannot have an eagle," she scolded.

Just then, there was another roll and crack. They both moved closer within inches away. Suddenly, a little beak broke though, then a little white head, and with a sudden crack, a baby eagle popped out, looking right at Silas. Mrs. Livingston was in shock to witness this little miracle. It was like nothing they ever watched before. Seeing chickens hatch was one thing. But watching an eagle came forth from an egg was a whole different adventure. Silas looked up at his mom.

"Mom, please."

She was so thrilled by the event. "Oh, well, okay. But only till it can fly. Then it goes back to the mountain. Agreed?"

"Agreed, Mom," said Silas. Silas looked up to heaven. "Thank you, Lord."

That night, Silas lay in bed thinking about the baby eagle and how he would care for it and all the fun he would have with his new friend. After all, how many kids get to own their own eagle? With these thoughts in his head, Silas closed his eyes and fell asleep.

CHAPTER 4

Silas's Newfound Friend

The next morning brought forth a beam of light that caught Silas square in the eyes. Like a bolt of lightning, he sprang from his bed, dressed, and darted down the hallway into the kitchen and out the back door toward the chicken coop.

Silas entered the coop very slowly to not frighten any of the chickens and moved gently toward the eagle. There it was with its fuzzy little body who had four chickens buzzing around it, wondering what this new, strange creature was. Silas just gazed at his new friend.

"Don't you worry about anything, little fella. I'm going to take care of you. I will help you to grow strong and healthy." And, looking toward heaven, he prayed, "Thank you, Lord, for this little creature that you gave. I will do my best to take care of this bird to when it can return to Eagle Mountain with the other eagles."

Just then, Mrs. Livingston came in; both just looked on as the little eagle wobbled about in the nest and chirped away.

"Well, Silas, you're a daddy. You need to get busy and do some research on eagles and what kind of food they eat," said Mrs. Livingston.

Silas then went out into the nearby field and came back with a handful of worms.

"Let's see if he likes these," said Silas. Putting one worm close to the eagle's beak, the baby eagle snatched it out his hand, looking for more. And so started Silas's journey with the baby eagle that would be the greatest adventure of his life.

CHAPTER 5

Raising the Baby Eagle

Two weeks had passed, and the eagle was getting around in the nest a lot easier now. He was still small and covered in peach fuzz, but the bird's energy and appetite were huge. The little bird could eat a whole dish of food and still want more. Silas managed the eagle's intake of food, making sure the bird did not overeat.

Silas had just finished his breakfast and was preparing the eagle's food, which he fed to the bird with an eyedropper. It was hard work, and Silas had to keep a constant watch on the baby eagle. As Silas filled the eyedropper and put it near the baby bird's mouth, the bird would open wide and let Silas squeezed the food down its tiny throat. Silas was amazed at how much he was learning about this tiny bird. It was a relationship that was being knit together with love that the two would hold close for the rest of their lives. The excitement Silas was feeling was too great for words. Even Silas's mother noticed that he had put his mind to something that really meant a lot to him. He was getting all his chores done and more around the house and farm. The responsibility Silas showed was outstanding.

The only thing that Mrs. Livingston was concerned about was that Silas wasn't playing with any of the other children in the area and that he might lose friends. The only friend who had any contact with him was a girl who lived just over the ridge. Her name was Betty Jo Stevens, and her parents had a farm that produces much of the wheat for the county. Betty Jo and Silas were close friends from birth, and if Silas had to tell anyone about the baby eagle, it would be Betty

Jo. They often went exploring together. Betty Jo knew all the paths in Eagle Mountain as well as Silas. If Silas was going to tell anyone about the baby eagle, it would be Betty Jo. She could keep a secret. Although he hadn't told Betty Jo about the eagle yet, he was waiting for the right time. The eagle was still very young, and Silas wanted to give all his attention to the baby eagle's welfare to make sure that it grew strong enough to get around on its own before he told anyone.

Silas had finished feeding the bird, and as he was cleaning up, he thought to himself, *Gee, I haven't even given him a name yet*. It had to be a name fitting for an eagle, one with strength and authority. Silas stood looking at the tiny bird in its nest. He could picture it fully grown, soaring through the air with its huge wing span sailing across the sky as if he owned it all to himself. One name stood out. A name his mother used to read about to him when she told him about some great Bible figures: Solomon, a name that expressed wisdom, knowledge, and understanding, strength, and authority.

"That's it. I'll call you Solomon, and when you're fully grown, you'll rule the sky," said Silas to the little bird.

The weeks ahead weren't coming soon enough for Silas before he could start training Solomon.

CHAPTER 6

Training the Baby Eagle

Twelve weeks had gone by, and by now, Solomon was starting to fledge. According to the books Silas was reading, it was almost time for his first flight. It was a beautiful sunny morning, and Silas and his mom were having breakfast and getting ready for the morning chores. As Silas placed his dish in the sink, there was a knock at the front door.

"I'll get it, Mom." Silas wiped his hands and went to open the door, and standing there, smiling, was Betty Jo. "Hi, Betty Jo, come on in. Have some breakfast with us," said Silas.

"Thank you, Silas, but I just ate breakfast. Hello, Mrs. Livingston. I came over to see if you and your mom are going to the town picnic this fall? The whole town is expected to show up," said Jo.

"Oh yeah! I forgot about it," replied Silas.

"I haven't seen you in weeks, Silas. Where have you been hiding? All the kids have been asking about you," asked Betty Jo.

"Well, you see, I've been pretty busy around here, you know, with the farm and things. There is a lot of responsibility running a farm," said Silas.

Betty Jo just stood there wide-eyed, looking at Silas and his mother, wondering if this was the same boy she explored with, climbed trees with, and swam with down at the old pond standing before her, talking about chores and responsibility. Just then, Betty

Jo turned to Mrs. Livingston and said, "Mrs. Livingston, am I in the right house?"

"Yes, dear, you're in the right house, I'm afraid. You see, Silas has become involved in a rather unusual pastime lately. Silas, I think it's time you showed Jo just what you have been up to these past weeks," replied Mrs. Livingston.

"Right, Mom, I think it's time Betty Jo knew about Solomon," said Silas.

"Solomon! Who is Solomon?" asked Betty Jo.

"You'll see. Come on out to the chicken house," replied Silas.

Silas took Betty Jo by the hand and led her out to the chicken house. Betty Jo was almost afraid to go in because she didn't know what to expect. As they got up to the chicken house door, Silas turned to Betty Jo and said, "Now whatever you see in here is our secret. My mom is the only other person who knows about Solomon. So swear you won't tell anyone."

"I swear I won't tell a soul, Silas." Betty Jo kept wondering who was Solomon.

So Silas took her into the chicken house. As they moved past all the chickens, there in front of her, perched up on a branch, sat Solomon, not fully grown yet but huge. His gray feathers were fledging. His piercing eyes were gazing right at her. Then, with a flutter of his wings, they almost reached from one side of the chicken house to the other. He sat there like a king on his thrown. Betty Jo stood in awe with her mouth wide open, just staring at this beautiful, huge bird, living in a chicken house. She could not believe what she was looking at.

"Silas, where, how did you ever?" Betty Jo tried to get the words out.

Silas sat her down and told her how he came to find the egg, hatch, and raise the baby eagle. She listened to his story about his Eagle Mountain adventure, the old Indian he met, hatching the egg, and raising the baby eagle up to now.

"Wow! Silas, I really give you a lot of credit for taking on a huge task like this. Not everyone gets to have a pet eagle."

As she watched how Silas handled the eagle with love and care, she knew that Solomon was the right name for him and that he was in the right home. She marveled at how Silas was able to put the bird on his arm and walk around like they were old buddies and how Solomon obeyed Silas's every command. Together, Silas and Betty Jo would become Solomon's parents, and in the weeks ahead, they would discover Solomon's special gift. Betty Jo was now just as committed to Solomon as Silas. And all three would become the closest of friends.

Three weeks had passed, and this was to be the morning of Solomon's first solo flight. His feathers had finished their fledging and were now bright and shined in the sun with beautiful shades of grays and whites. Both Silas and Betty Jo were up early and ready to see Solomon off. They didn't have to worry about him flying off too far because as Solomon was concerned, this was his home and where he would return.

"Well, this is it, Betty Jo, the day Solomon becomes king of the sky," said Silas.

"Yeah, I feel like how a mother must feel, sending her child off on his first day of school," replied Betty Jo.

They took Solomon to a small clearing not far from the farm. It was a clear, sunny day with a slight breeze blowing in from the east, just the right day for a flight. Silas and Betty Jo were careful to make sure that no one was around. This was a top-secret mission. The less people who knew about Solomon, the better. Silas would pick his own time to tell anyone else about the bird. He was afraid they would want to put Solomon in a zoo or worse.

Betty Jo saw someone coming toward them in the distance. They couldn't see who was the person getting closer, then Silas saw that it was his mother. Mrs. Livingston came to see Solomon's first flight. She knew how important this was to Silas, and she wasn't about to miss this for the world.

"Hi, Mom, come to see the blast off the USS Solomon?" said Silas.

"You bet, I wouldn't miss this for anything," replied Mrs. Livingston.

"I guess your real proud of Silas, Mrs. Livingston," said Jo.

"Yes, I am, Betty Jo. He put a lot of hard work and effort into raising Solomon. He has become quite the responsible young man," replied Mrs. Livingston.

Silas stood there, blushing and taking it all in. Even Solomon looked a little proud of himself, sitting there on Silas's arm. Mrs. Livingston and Betty Jo just looked at each other and smiled.

"Well, let's get this show on the road you guys," said Mrs. Livingston.

"Right, Mom. The time has come for you to show your stuff, Solomon, so let's do it," said Silas.

There was a small hill at the edge of the clearing. Silas took Solomon to the top of the hill. He figured this would be a good starting point for the bird to begin his first flight; should he have to land, there wouldn't be any brush or large trees in the way, so Solomon could land in the clearing without hurting himself. Mrs. Livingston and Betty Jo stayed at the center of the clearing so they could ready if Solomon landed near them. It was at this time that Silas, with Solomon resting on his arm, knelt down and prayed, "Dear Lord, I pray that you just give Solomon the strength and power to fly as you intended for him to do, for you made him. And I thank you, Lord, for giving me this special friend. And I thank you, Lord, for a mom so understanding and a friend like Betty Jo, so trusting to help me in raising and training Solomon. Amen."

Then as Silas rose to his feet, he looked toward the sky and, with a great thrust of his arm, threw Solomon into the air. Like the great giant king he was, Solomon soared through the air. His great wing span glided into the wind, reaching for the clouds as he took command of the air and claimed his territory in the sky. Silas stood like a proud father watching his baby walk for the first time. Mrs. Livingston just gazed at this marvel with tears in her eyes, feeling for her son and the monarch she was watching, soaring above her head in the sky. Betty Jo watched with goose bumps as Solomon glided across the sky, riding the wind with a smile a million words could never describe.

The scene taking place in that small clearing was something out of a fairytale, and only the people in it standing there, watching the sight over their heads, could ever feel the thrill and excitement that only they were meant to witness this day in history.

Silas, sitting down on top of the hill with his arms wrapped around his knees, watched as Solomon took over the sky. For Silas, it was to be the first part of Solomon's training. For Mrs. Livingston, it was seeing her son became a man. For Betty Jo, it was seeing a part of Silas she had never seen and growing closer to him for it. For Solomon, it was the beginning of life for which he was meant to be, a life of discovery and adventure for this king of the sky.

C H A P T E R   7

The Eagle's Size

It was now about five weeks since Solomon's first flight at the clearing, and the bird was doing amazingly well. Silas had him flying every day all over the farm and surrounding territory but always keeping close to home so as not to arouse any suspicion. Solomon always returned home like a homing pigeon. The training and time that went into Solomon was paying off.

It was midafternoon, and Silas was busy cleaning the chicken house. Although his eagle training took up much of his time, he still had his household chores to do. Mrs. Livingston had her own share of the work to do also, which was to inspect the eggs before shipping them to town. The Livingston supplied about 5 0 percent of the eggs to their little community. All was busy this day around the Livingston farm when suddenly, from out of the barn, there came a crashing sound. Silas looked up and gazed over at the barn. Mrs. Livingston came running out from the chicken house, wiping her hands in her apron. Both Silas and his mother walked to the center of the yard, staring at the barn.

"Did you hear that crash, Mom?" asked Silas.

"Yes, I did. It sounded like it came from the barn," replied Mrs. Livingston.

"Do you think it's those wild dogs coming down from the hills again?"

"Could be, son. You better go get the scattergun," said his mother.

"Right, Mom."

Silas ran off to the house and soon returned with a twelve-gauge shotgun. The county had been having problems with wild dogs lately, and some nearby farms were losing cattle and sheep. Getting rid of wild dogs was no easy job since they usually traveled in packs of ten and twelve. And for a mother and her young son, it was at these times that Mrs. Livingston wished there was a man around the house. As Silas and his mother moved closer to the barn door, they could hear rustling going on inside. The closer they got, the louder the noise became. It sounded like boxes and things being knocked over. Slowly, they crept up to the barn door, Silas holding the scattergun and Mrs. Livingston holding on to Silas's shoulders. Silas could feel his hands sweating, ready to shoot the first thing that came through that door. Just then, Silas remembered that Solomon was in there. The chicken house was too small for him, so he built a big perch in the barn using some fallen oak branches. What they didn't know was if Solomon had any company in there with him. Silas turned to his mother and said in a low voice, "Mom, Solomon is in there."

"Well, son, let's hope and pray nothing else is," replied his mother.

"I'll open the door, and go in first, Mom, and you be ready to go for help," said Silas.

Silas then crept up slowly to the barn door and grabbed hold of the latch and opened the door with a quick pull. Standing there with his gun aimed inside the doorway, Silas looked all around, walking in slowly. Then, as he turned his head toward the place where Solomon's perch was, he stood straight up and saw that the oak branch was broken in half. But where was Solomon? There didn't seem to be any sign of wild dogs, only some bales of hay knocked over. Silas relaxed a little and lowered his gun. Mrs. Livingston called from outside the barn, "Silas, is everything all right? Are you all right, son?"

Silas stood there scanning the entire barn, looking for anything unusual. Then he looked up to the rafters of the barn, and there, seated on one of the huge old beams, was Solomon. His wings spread out, almost touching each side of the barn, and his noble head was staring down at Silas. Silas stood there for a minute, gazing up at this huge bird. His mother came behind him, and seeing her son looking up, the two marveled at Solomon's size, something they both hadn't noticed before, for he looked bigger than any normal eagle. They had both seen eagles at the zoo and flying overhead near Eagle Mountain, but it seemed as though Solomon's wing span reached over fourteen feet, and he was still a young bird by normal standards. Then Mrs. Livingston, looking over at Solomon's perch, realized what that sound was. It was the sound of Solomon's perch breaking from under his weight.

But all this didn't seem right. That was a huge oak branch, one of the hardest woods around. How could it break so easily? They both looked up at Solomon. His huge wing span stretched out across the rafters, and for the first time, his screeching voice vibrated the walls of the barn.

Mrs. Livingston knew that the time was coming that Silas would have a difficult choice to make: to let Solomon go and live on his own. What she didn't know was how to tell Silas.

The Town Picnic

The day had come at last for the town picnic. Everyone in town was getting ready. Many were baking pies and making fried chicken and salads and all kinds of deserts. There would be prizes for the best-looking hog and horse and cow. There will be games and rides for all ages with lots of fun to last the whole day.

It was a beautiful morning, and everything was going perfectly. Silas sprang out of bed, happy as a lark. He fumbled over his own feet as he went over to the window to catch a breath of fresh air and take in all the beauty of the farm and surrounding hills as Mother Nature awoke and showed off her splendor in the early morning light. Silas popped his head out the window and said, "Thank you, Lord, for this great day." He made record timing getting dressed as he slipped into his trousers and pulled his shirt over his head. From the kitchen, Mrs. Livingston could hear the fumbling going on in Silas's room, and she could only smile as she prepared breakfast.

"Silas, breakfast is ready. Hurry or your pancakes will get cold."

"I'll be right there, Mom. Don't let those pancakes get away," replied Silas.

As he entered the kitchen, the smell of the hot pancakes filled the air, and Silas was taken in by its aroma, then, sitting down at the table, he inhaled the freshly made pancakes, taking the maple syrup and drenching the pancakes in a sea of goodness.

"Well, you're sure in a happy mood this morning," said Mrs. Livingston.

"And why not, Mom? It's the day of the town picnic, isn't it? Where else can a guy go to get so many hot dogs and hamburgers and beans and ice cream and—"

"Okay, okay, Silas, I get the idea," said Mrs. Livingston, laughing.

"It's too bad Solomon couldn't go to the picnic. Can you imagine if me and Betty Jo came flying in on Solomon's back and landed right in the middle of the picnic grounds?"

"Well, I think Solomon is better staying right where he is today, Silas. Remember, you, Betty Jo, and me are the only people who know about Solomon. And it has to stay that way. He'll be all right for one day without you," said Mrs. Livingston.

"I guess you're right, Mom. I mean, I can't always be around him to protect him, and a guy has to have some time to himself, right?" said Silas as he looked out the door to see Betty Jo coming up the road.

Mrs. Livingston saw the same look on Silas's face and realized her son was indeed growing up and starting to think about other things beside farm life and a giant eagle.

"Before you start getting independent on me and Solomon, young man, you have chores to do first," said Mrs. Livingston.

Silas lost a bit of his smile, but he didn't mind doing his chores today. In fact, as soon as he finished his breakfast, he darted out the door to meet Betty Jo, and they both went off together.

Mrs. Livingston, watching from the kitchen window, noticed a new interest in her son's life now: Betty Jo. Smiling, she continued doing her dishes as she watched the two off. Silas never gave his mother any trouble when it came to doing work around the house. He was a very responsible boy, something he got from his father. His mother had to only tell him once, and it was done. She could see how much work Silas had put into raising Solomon over the past few months, and she could see that her boy was growing up.

Silas and Betty Jo entered the barn to where Solomon was perched high in the rafters. Looking up at his friend, Silas said, "Looks like you're on your own today, my friend. Hope you don't mind, but we have a picnic to go to. Wish I could bring you, but you may scare some people there. They aren't used to seeing a giant eagle crashing the picnic."

"Yeah, it would be a little more than crashing," said Betty Jo, laughing.

Solomon just stared down from his loft at his friend, giving some occasional loud chirps to signify he understood what Silas was saying.

"I'll see you when I get back, Solomon. I guess we both need a little time to ourselves. So you be good while I'm gone, okay? And I'll be back soon."

Then Silas turned and, with a little kick in the dirt, slowly walked out of the barn with Betty Jo, turning back one more time to wave goodbye to his friend. Then Betty Jo turned to Silas and said, "Silas, I have to go home and get some things together for the picnic. Come by and pick me up, okay?"

"Okay, Betty Jo."

Then she kissed him on the cheek and ran off down the road. Silas's heart felt like it was going a mile a minute as he watched his best friend scurry on down the road. Meanwhile, Mrs. Livingston watched from the kitchen window.

"Silas, it's almost time to go. Come on in and get washed up. We don't want to be late for the picnic," called Mrs. Livingston.

"I'll be right there, Mom. I'll be right there."

He kept his eye on Jo as she got farther down the road. As Silas came strolling in the kitchen, his mother just watched as he walked on by as if in a trance toward his room and down the hallway; all she could do from crying was watch Silas stroll on by with not only a giant bird on his hands but now a woman on his hands.

Soon they were loading the car, getting ready to head to the picnic grounds.

"Mom, can we pick up Betty Jo on the way?" asked Silas.

"Sure, we can, Silas. Sure, we can," replied Mrs. Livingston with a smile.

As they made their way down the road toward the Steven's farm to pick up Betty Jo, Mrs. Livingston noticed that Silas was quiet.

"Worried about our feathered friend back there?"

"A little, Mom. He's never really been alone like this. Do you think he'll be all right by himself?" asked Silas.

"I think so, son. He can take care of himself if need be. All birds have to learn to fend for themselves, Silas. It's no different for Solomon," replied Mrs. Livingston. Then, in her motherly wisdom, she looked at Silas and said, "Silas, someday, he will have to be set free. You can't hold on to him forever."

"I know, Mom. I know. I just hope I have the courage to let him go when the time comes," replied Silas.

As they drove along, Silas could see Eagle Mountain in the distance. He knew one day Solomon would have to return home. There he would truly be the king of the mountain.

*****

The Steven's farm was just ahead, and they could see Betty Jo standing outside, waiting on the porch, waving with a big smile on her face. Silas perked up when he saw Betty Jo, and Mrs. Livingston noticed his reaction also when he spotted her. *It's going to be an interesting picnic*, she thought to her herself, grinning and shaking her head as she drove on.

"Look, Mom, it's Betty Jo. That's what I like, a girl who's on time," said Silas.

As they pulled up to the front porch, Silas popped his head out the window. "Hi, Betty Jo, all ready to go? You look great."

"Thanks, Silas. Hello, Mrs. Livingston," replied Betty Jo.

"Hi, Jo, you do look lovely, Betty Jo. What did you do with your hair?" said Mrs. Livingston.

Silas, turning around in his seat, looked at Betty Jo in a whole new way. Her hair was all golden, long and hanging over her shoulders. She had on a little makeup, lipstick, and a beautiful blue dress. He had never seen her like this before. As he stared at her, he could feel his heart racing a mile a minute again. "You're beautiful, Betty Jo," said Silas.

Betty Jo just motioned back "thank you" to Silas with her lips, then smiled. Mrs. Livingston kept her eyes on the road.

As they rolled along, they could see the picnic grounds up ahead. The church steeple was in clear view down the road, and some people were already there setting up tables and chairs and placing food and drinks. There were children running around, playing tag, and some barbecues were smoking up a storm. Silas and Betty Jo were bouncing up and down in the car excitedly. Mrs. Livingston didn't mind at all. She knew that Silas needed this time to just be a kid and to forget about his responsibilities at home. She didn't want him growing too fast for he still had his childhood to enjoy first.

Meanwhile, back at the barn, Solomon was getting a bit bewildered. He had to stretch his wings and get out of the barn and fly. Being locked inside the barn made him edgy. Where was Silas? Why didn't he come today? His curiosity got the best of him when he saw at the other end of the barn that the two hay loft doors were left open. From his perch, Solomon could smell the fresh, clean air of the outdoors, and with one great leap from his perch, he soared across the rafters of the barn and out through the hay loft doors and into the crisp, clean country sky. His great wing span carried him over the tree tops and valleys as Solomon enjoyed a spell of freedom while his friend was away.

Meanwhile, back at the picnic, Silas and Betty Jo were enjoying themselves, playing tag with a few of the other town's kids. Mrs. Livingston was busy helping the other women with refreshments and chatting with the pastor's wife about things on the farm. The picnic had been well under way now for about two hours, and everyone was having a good time and enjoying themselves, leaving all their cares back on the farms. The picnic grounds were by the church, which had a river that ran along the banks of the church grounds. It was a very active river with a very strong current and rapids. The river ran into Whitney Falls, an eighty-foot-high falls, which then fed the smaller rivers along the countryside. It was a perfect day for a picnic, and the whole town was here. There were games, racing, eating, singing, prizes, and lots of fun.

Silas and Betty Jo were well into their game of tag when Silas decided the best place to be where he would not get tagged was out on a big branch of a maple tree that hung out over the river's edge.

The river current was running very fast this day, and from the shore, one could reach out and touch the white caps breaking over the rocks that lay along the river's edge. As Silas sat on the branch looking down at the other kids chasing one another, there came the sound of a crack. The branch suddenly dropped out from below him about ten inches. Silas froze, and the other kids stopped in their tracks. Betty Jo turned and saw that Silas's weight was causing the branch to give way.

"Silas! Don't move, don't move an inch," Betty Jo yelled.

All the other kids stopped playing, and some girls screamed. This caused the grown-ups to look, and everyone could see Silas on the verge of falling into the river. Mrs. Livingston looked over where the commotion was and screamed when she saw Silas, dropping a bowl of potato salad and running over to her son, now perch on a broken branch, ready fall into the raging river. She was soon joined by the whole town, shouting to Silas not to move.

Meanwhile, Solomon was flying high up in the clouds over Eagle Mountain, enjoying his freedom. But something within him told him something was not right. He quickly descended and soared over farms and fields, following his instincts.

Silas sat perched out on the branch, trying to remain calm when all of a sudden, there came another crack. Everyone screamed. Betty Jo stood in horror, holding Mrs. Livingston. Then, with one great crack, the branch broke free from the tree, and down they both went into the rapids. Swiftly, Silas was carried away downstream, yelling for help. Some of the men climbed out on other branches hanging upside down, trying to grab Silas as he went passed them. But the river was too fast, and the boy went by the outstretched arms of the men. The cold water carried Silas through huge rocks and downed trees as he gasped for air. The whole town was now in a state of horror for not far ahead was Whitney Falls. If Silas reached the falls, he'd be doomed.

All watched as Silas came closer and closer to the edge of the falls. The eighty-foot drop would dash him on the rocks below. As he tried desperately to grab onto something, the strong current just carried him closer to his doom. He was now out in the middle of the river where no one could reach him. His mother was now on her knees crying and calling for her son while women tried to comfort her. Betty Jo was next to her with her hand on her shoulder, crying. The town, getting ready to witness the boy's death, could do nothing but watch as Silas neared the edge of the falls. And as all stood holding one another and watching as the boy went over the edge, all screamed and put their hands over their faces when suddenly, up from the falls, came the mighty sight of a giant eagle, and in his talons, he carried Silas.

Someone cried out, "Look! Look at that! What is that? He has Silas."

Everyone stood in there amazement.

Mrs. Livingston rose to her feet and yelled "Solomon, Solomon" as the giant bird circled around the picnic grounds, the crowd standing in disbelief. Solomon soon came to a slow descent and, landing in the middle of the grounds, gently set Silas on the ground and, with a loud screech, spread his huge wings and then lowered his head to his friend. Mrs. Livingston and Betty Jo both ran over to Solomon and threw their arms around his neck, kissing and holding him. Mrs. Livingston held Silas in her arms as the whole town looked on at this scene, keeping their distance and wondering with mouths wide open.

Mrs. Livingston, standing next to the giant bird, holding Silas and Betty Jo in her arms, looked at the townspeople and said, "I guess you're all wondering about this. Well, now that it is no secret. I should explain about Solomon and just how he came to be our friend. Let's all gather in the church, and Silas, Betty Jo, and I will tell you all about it."

So the whole town went over to the church, and Silas told them the story of how he found the eagle's egg, hatched it, and raised the baby eagle. How he grew to be so big was a mystery, but Silas told them he thought it had something to do with the testing of the atomic bomb that took place. Some of the boys and girls looked out the window as Solomon perched himself on top of the church swing set. Mrs. Livingston told them that he was very gentle, that he only stayed around the farm, and that Silas and Betty Jo had complete control over him. He wasn't a danger to anyone as Solomon displayed by saving Silas's life. They are committed to each other.

One of the people stood and asked, "How do we know that Solomon will stay by your farm and not come into town and wreak havoc someday?"

"The only reason Solomon came this far today was because he sensed that I was in danger. That's the only reason he left the farm," said Silas.

Then the pastor stepped forward and said, "I think everyone here should thank the good Lord that Solomon was around to save this boy. I think we should all go home now, and perhaps we should have a town meeting this week to discuss this matter further. Given the fact that the bird doesn't seem to be a threat and as I watch him sitting on that swing set out there, it seems Silas and Betty Jo here have done a pretty good job raising Solomon thus far and also given the fact that Solomon is already, judging from the size of him, about four to five months old and we haven't had any problems so far with him. Let's all go home and consider the matter."

With that, everyone rose and wished Silas well and started out of the church for home. No one seemed to be afraid of the bird as they walked past him sitting up on the swing set. All just stared at Solomon. Kids were smiling and pointing, others just staring in wonder.

CHAPTER 9

The Wild Dogs

It was now a week since the town picnic, and the Livingston farm was the main topic of the county. Every day, someone was knocking on the door from a newspaper to write an article on Solomon and Silas or someone from some society wanting to do a study on the bird and his size. There were offers from zoos all over the country who wanted to purchase Solomon for a great deal of money, which would put Silas and his mother on easy street. But it wasn't fame and fortune that Silas wanted. All he wanted was for Solomon to be free and happy. He didn't want him caged up in some zoo, studied like some science project. Mrs. Livingston had hardly any time to do her house chores because of Solomon's fame. She too wanted Solomon to be free and happy.

It was a rainy day, and Silas and Betty Jo sat with Solomon up in the barn loft, wondering what was to become of their friend. Both sat with long faces and heavy hearts with their feet hanging over the hay loft, looking out at the rain dripping off the edge of the barn. Mrs. Livingston stood out on the porch, looking at the barn. She knew Silas and Betty Jo were in there. Picking up the umbrella by the door, she headed over to the barn. Once inside, she could Silas and Betty Jo sitting up in the hay loft. She went over to the ladder and climbed up to join them. Sitting down next to Silas with her legs hanging out, watching the rain, all three just took in the beautiful landscape surrounding the farm, watching the raindrops as they pounded the dirt and made puddles in the road.

"I don't know what to do, Mom. Now that everyone knows about Solomon, they all want a part of him. They all think they have a right to him as if they knew what was best for him," said Silas.

"I know, Silas, but you're going to have to make a decision soon. Yes, they all want a part of him. I guess that's human nature. What do you think is best for him, son?" asked Mrs. Livingston.

Silas turned to Betty Jo. She didn't have to say anything. They both knew the answer. Solomon had to be set free—to live on Eagle Mountain where he belonged. There no one would own him. He could be the king of that mountain. They both see in the faint distance through the rain the clouded image of Eagle Mountain.

"The pastor came today. He said that the town council is talking about putting Solomon in a zoo," said Mrs. Livingston.

"What! They can't do that, Mom. He doesn't belong to them. He belongs to me. I raised him. I'll never let them take him. I can hide him in places they will never find him," replied Silas.

"And just where are you going to hide a giant eagle the size of Solomon? Sooner or later, they will come for him, and they will probably have the sheriff with them when they do. There is still some time. They haven't said when this was going to happen, but you have to decide soon. Solomon's life depends on it now," said Mrs. Livingston.

Betty Jo placed her hand on Silas's shoulder. "Your mom is right, Silas. It's Solomon we have to think of."

Mrs. Livingston got up and climbed down the ladder and walked out of the barn toward the house. Silas and Betty Jo just sat there. Both knew what had to be done. Both remained silent.

Two minutes later, the silence was broken by a scream from Silas's mother. Silas and Betty Jo jumped up and climbed down the ladder like mountain goats. Running out the barn door, it caught them both by surprise when they saw Mrs. Livingston frozen in her tracks, staring at two wild dogs that had wandered down from the mountains, both hungry and looking for food. They had her cornered between the front door and the driveway. Betty Jo started throwing rocks at the dogs, but that just made them growl and bark, standing their ground. Mrs. Livingston could feel her heart pounding in her chest a mile a minute with thoughts of horror going through her mind. As she turned slowly and saw Silas and Betty Jo just behind her, she said to Silas in a very low voice, "Go and get the scattergun, son. Move very slow and try not to excite them."

Silas then walked toward the house, keeping his eyes on the dogs. Once inside, he grabbed the gun and started to put two shells in. Meanwhile, Mrs. Livingston and Betty Jo stayed perfectly still, waiting for Silas to come flying out the door, blasting. Just then, as Silas came bursting through the door, the gun in his hands ready to shoot, he tripped coming down the steps. He could feel his legs going out from under him. The gun went flying, and when it hit the ground, it blew a hole through the barn door, sending the dogs into a frenzy barking and growling.

Betty Jo stood frozen, trying not to move. Mrs. Livingston backed up slowly, falling backward to the ground and screamed. The dogs started moving in for the kill, teeth showing, moving in closer and closer. Then both dogs perked up when they heard a piercing sound from above, and suddenly landing between Mrs. Livingston and the two dogs was Solomon, wings outstretched and ready for a fight. The dogs tried to get close, but every time they got within the distance of Solomon's mighty beak, he took a piece of them. Each time they tried, Solomon sent them back. Silas, now getting to his feet, ran and grabbed the gun and, aiming at the dogs, fired one shot, just missing one of the dogs. But it sent them running for the hills. Solomon at last calmed down, turning his great head toward Mrs. Livingston to make sure she was okay. Silas ran over to his mother to help her up.

"Are you all right, Mom?"

"Yes, I'm all right now. Thank you, son. You were very brave, and you my fine-feathered friend, you saved my life." She wrapped her arms around Solomon's neck and kissed him.

Betty Jo ran up to Solomon also and gave him a big hug, then gave Silas and Mrs. Livingston a great big hug. "I was so frightened. That was so close," cried Betty Jo.

"It's okay, Betty Jo. Thanks to our two brave men here, I don't think those dogs will come back here too soon," replied Mrs. Livingston.

Then Silas held Solomon and said, "How can anybody want to put you in a zoo, old friend? But don't you worry because that is never going to happen. You better go back into the barn now, Solomon. Go on. I'll be there in a little while," said Silas.

And then the giant bird spread his wings, and off he went, up and over to the other side of the barn and disappeared. Silas, Betty Jo, and Mrs. Livingston walked over to the porch to catch their breaths. Betty Jo ran in the house and soon returned with some water. All three sat on the porch, sipping their water, pondering what just happened. Mrs. Livingston was now more confused about the fate of Solomon. He had already saved her son once from death and now her from wild dogs. She wasn't going to let anything worry her now. She would just leave it in the Lord's hands now. She knew Silas would make the right decision when the time came. Mrs. Livingston got up and went into the house, leaving Silas and Betty Jo sitting on the steps.

Silas sat looking out toward Eagle Mountain. There were low clouds just below the summit now from the rain. It looked like a lost city on a cloud. "I wish we had never gone to that picnic, then I wouldn't have fallen into that river, and Solomon would still be a secret," said Silas.

"Don't do that to yourself, Silas. You couldn't have known what would happen at the picnic. Let's just thank God Solomon was there to save you. What if that would have happened if you never brought that egg down from the mountain? It had to be the Lord who caused you to go up there. And it had to be the Lord who brought that storm. And it had to be the Lord who kept that egg in one piece for you to get it in to the chicken house to hatch. Who else do you know who has done what you have done these past few months? And who knew Solomon would grow four times the size of a normal eagle? Only the Lord. But you are probably right. It must have been from that bomb test. The mother must have gotten caught up in the fall-out. That's why you found her dead nearby when you discovered the eggs," replied Betty Jo.

"Boy, Betty Jo, can you imagine if I was able to get all three eggs down?"

They both just looked to heaven and, at the same time, said, "Oh! Boy!"

Soon Mrs. Livingston came out and said, "How about something to eat, kids? I have some great fried chicken with mash potatoes and greens and nice cold root beer pop."

They both jumped up from the steps, yelling, "Oh! Boy!" And into the kitchen they ran.

As Mrs. Livingston and Betty Jo placed the food on the table, Silas just stared out at the barn. He had a thousand things going through his head about Solomon and the bird's future. They all took their place at the table, and Betty Jo said to Silas, "You pray, Silas." Which instantly took his mind off his troubles and back to the Lord where they belonged.

"Dear Lord, we thank you for this food and everything you have done for my mom, Betty Jo, and me. Thank you for bringing Solomon into our lives, and I pray your protection over him and also over us as you have already shown through Solomon. Help me to make the right decision for him, Lord. Amen."

As they helped themselves to the food, Mrs. Livingston said to Silas, "I'm sure the Lord will help you, Silas, and Solomon. After all, he is one of God's own creatures."

"I know he will, Mom. But it's getting crazy in town. Everywhere I go, people come up to me and want to talk about Solomon. Even at school, the kids all want me to bring him to school like we were talking about a pet hamster or something. Everyone in town knows about him. I hate going anywhere. They're asking me where he came from, and I can't tell them exactly where because there will be all kinds of people going to Eagle Mountain trying to catch giant eagles. They don't know that Solomon is one of a kind. And when he dies, there aren't any more like him. Even if he finds a mate, it doesn't mean he will have giant baby eagles. Most likely, they will be normal-sized. You'd think we had King Kong living on our farm."

Mrs. Livingston reached over and placed her hand on Silas's shoulder and, with a little smile said, "Well, thank God he's not King Kong. I don't know where we would get all the bananas to feed him."

They all laughed and finished their dinner. After dinner, Mrs. Livingston drove Betty Jo home. Silas went out to the barn and climbed up to sit with Solomon. The boy sat stroking the bird's long neck feathers as two friends watched the full moon come up over Eagle Mountain. Solomon seemed to almost moan at the moon as if he were saying, "I want to go home."

"Don't worry, Solomon. The Lord will find a way. No one is going to take you anywhere you don't want to go. But I think we both know where you belong."

The silhouetted Eagle Mountain behind the full moon in front of them.

The Flight in the Sky

Mrs. Livingston walked slowly down the hallway toward Silas's room to peek in. He was fast asleep with the covers pulled up to his chin. But if she could see into his dream, she would see her young adventurer riding high in the sky on the back of his giant eagle, soaring over mountains and flying down just inches over raging rivers. She would see the beautiful countryside with its rolling hills and farms scattered about from a height of five hundred feet. If she could see her son's dream, there would be no cares or worries as he held on to Solomon's neck with his hair blowing in the wind, flying alongside a flock of geese, gazing upon all of God's creation, seen through the eyes of an eagle.

But Silas's dream was only the beginning for this young explorer. His heart was telling him that dreams could come true if you really believed and wanted them to. Mrs. Livingston tiptoed over to Silas's bedside to kiss him on his forehead. As she looked at her son sleeping and looked at some of the model airplanes he built that were all over his room, she whispered to him, "Someday, my son, you will fly like your eagle friend. I know you will." Then she quietly left, and turning to close the door, she threw one last kiss.

The next morning was a brisk one. The wind blew at a steady five miles per hour out of the west across the county. There were only a few small clouds hanging in the clear-blue sky. Silas had finished his breakfast and did his morning chores. It was eleven o'clock, and Silas and Solomon were now rested atop Hunter's Ridge, a high point in the county but only a short distance from their farm. As the two looked out over the area, Silas could see Betty Jo's farm and some other small homes scattered across the valley. His heart was racing like a galloping horse. All he could think about as he stood next to his seven-foot-high friend was gliding over everything he cast his eye upon. Silas knew that Solomon could easily carry his weight. As Silas pondered all these thoughts, his adventurous blood was beginning to boil. The wind was right. The sky was clear. It was the perfect time for flying. Silas put his arms around his giant friend and said, "Well, my friend, ready to take a passenger aboard for a flight in the sky?" Solomon gave a little push with his beak to signify, "Hop on." Silas knew he could trust Solomon with his life. Silas climbed up on Solomon's great neck and held on to his feathers. Then, with one command, Silas said, "Up and away!"

With one great thrust of the eagle's wings, they rose off the ground and up into the air. Silas held on tight as the ground got further and further away, and the clouds got nearer and nearer. His heart was now beating faster as they flew out over the edge of Hunter's Ridge and glided across the valley above the trees and soaring past farms.

As they approached Betty Jo's farm, he could see Betty Jo in the horse corral with a colt.

"Let's go say hello, Solomon."

The bird banked, and down they went flying just over the corral. Then, suddenly, Betty Jo could hear her name being called. She looked up, and falling back, there was Silas flying with the eagle. All she could do was laugh in delight and excitement for her friend. Silas waved to Betty Jo as he flew by.

As Solomon's mighty wings flapped faster and faster, he increased in speed, and soon they were soaring high and over the town. Main Street was busy with people and cars moving around as usual. No one took notice of them as they soared high above. Silas was ecstatic as the wind splashed against his face and his hair, blowing in the coolness of the air. The sight was breathtaking. He could see the entire countryside with all its farmhouses and cattle and sheep as they grazed in the pastures. He could see the river at its full length with all its winding turns and waterfalls.

Off in the distance, Silas could see Twin Peaks, the highest mountains in the county. Both peaks were snowcapped with little clouds just below the peaks. It was like a painting on a canvas. Silas was living his dream. He just held on and inhaled every sight and sound as they both sailed over treetops and hills; descending toward the town, Silas decided to fly right down the center of Main Street where everyone could see. Since they all knew about Solomon, they might as well knew what he could do. This was the busy shopping center of town with people coming and going in and out of stores and shops. This was the perfect time.

As they got closer to the beginning of town, Solomon started his descent, wings outstretched, coming in faster and faster. Just then, Mrs. Johnson came walking out of the butcher shop when she looked up and saw a sight and screamed, "Good heavens, look."

All looked down the center of Main Street to see Silas sitting on the giant eagle, flying ten feet off the ground, soaring right down the center of town. Jaws were dropped, and mouths were wide open. As they passed overhead, some hats went flying, and newspapers went flying up in the air. The whole town watched as Silas flew Solomon like he was riding his horse.

The butcher standing by said to some people nearby, "That boy sure did tame that bird. I never seen anything like that before in my life. I hope he doesn't hurt himself riding that bird like that."

"I wonder if his mother knows what he is up to, riding that bird right down the center of town like that," replied Mrs. Johnson.

Silas kept on going right past everyone until he reached the end of town, and as all watched, he disappeared over the treetops and out of sight. Silas and Solomon were the talk of the town. The rescue at the picnic was still fresh in everyone's mind, and now this gave the town something else to talk about.

In a few days after Silas's joyride down Main Street, the town started filling up with newspaper people who wanted a story about the giant bird. Now Silas regretted ever taking that flight. He didn't think it would attract so much attention. Mrs. Livingston kept the gate closed at the road that led up to the farm so reporters couldn't get in.

As Mrs. Livingston and Silas sat at the dinner table, things were quiet as they ate until Mrs. Livingston said, "That was a very dumb thing to do, Silas, flying though the center of town like that. Now we have every reporter trying to get to us. We can't even go into town to buy food without being overpowered by newspaper people. What made you do something so crazy as to jump on Solomon's back and go for a joyride? Do you realize you could have fallen off and fell hundreds of feet to the ground and been killed?" Mrs. Livingston began to cry just thinking about what could have happened.

Silas went over to his mother and put his hand on her shoulder, saying, "I'm sorry, Mom. I just wanted to see what it was like to see the world from Solomon's eyes. But I'm okay, and I promise, Mom, that I won't ever try that again."

"Please don't. You had better get ready for bed now, Silas," replied Mrs. Livingston.

"Yes, Mom."

Silas headed down the hall, realizing how much he had hurt his mother and the anguish he put her through. She already lost one man in the family, and now she came close to losing another. He came to his bedroom door, turning to see his mother still sitting at the table with her hands covering her face. It was a hard lesson learned about taking risk where more than one person could get hurt.

That night, Silas sat by his bedroom window looking up at the stars, thinking about the words to pray, so he just told the Lord, "Dear Lord, forgive me for being such a knucklehead. Mom was right. I could have been killed or hurt someone else in town. If something happened to me, Mom would be all alone on this farm with no one to help her. It was just something I had to do. But I won't be doing that again. So I'm asking you, Lord, to give me better judgment and wisdom when it comes to Solomon. I didn't even think of him and what would happen if anything happened to me. I guess the town would have decided his fate. So please, Lord, keep your hand upon my mom and me and Solomon and over this farm. Thank you, Lord. Amen." So Silas climbed into bed, closed his eyes, and fell asleep. That night, he didn't dream about flying on eagles.

CHAPTER 11

Suspicions of the Eagle

Two weeks had passed at the Livingston farm, and all was pretty normal. Mrs. Livingston was busy in the chicken house, checking eggs and cleaning the chicken boxes. Silas was mending a fence that a horse had knocked over by the corral. Solomon was resting quietly, perched up on his branch in the barn.

The same couldn't be said for the Smith Cattle Ranch five miles down the road. Mr. Smith was coming out the front door, holding a cup of coffee and smelling the fresh morning air and feeling great. Mrs. Smith soon joined her husband on the porch, also holding her coffee as they both inhaled the new day.

"I think I'll go down to the pasture mother and check on our babies," said Mr. Smith, referring to their prize cows.

"You do that, dear. Don't walk too fast down there now. Your blood pressure, you know."

"Yes, mother, I'll take my time. It's a beautiful day anyway. I may as well enjoy it on the way there," replied Mr. Smith.

The Smiths were kind, old folks in their midseventies. Mr. Smith was a retired doctor, a bit overweight, with a full head of white hair and small white beard. Mrs. Smith was a retired schoolteacher, slim, and always wore her hair up with her glasses still hanging around her neck as she did in class.

Mr. Smith took his time walking along the road down to the pasture, stopping every once in a while to smell the roses that grew wild along the road. They were everywhere, and the aroma just made one feel that it was going to be a great day. That was until he got closer to the wooden gate that enclosed the five acres of the fine grazing pasture for his five prize cows.

As he opened the gate and walked in, he could see out in the grass the cows chewing away under a tall maple tree. He didn't think too much of anything until he noticed that there were only four cows. *She must have wandered off on her own to another part of the pasture*, he thought to himself. So he decided to go look for the missing cow. Now five acres was a lot to cover for a man in his seventies, so he often sat down on a large rock to rest. It took the better part of two hours, but after searching the whole five acres, there was no sign of her. Mr. Smith stood by the gate, wondering what could have happened. Did someone come at night and steal his prize cow? After all, a cow is not a light thing to carry away.

As he walked back to the house to tell his wife, it suddenly dawned on him: that eagle. That eagle was the only animal large enough to pick up a cow. Now it was time to call the sheriff.

Meanwhile, a few miles from the Smith's ranch, Mr. Downing, the towns local hog farmer, was just finishing his coffee and heading out toward the hog pen. Mr. Downing had many hogs but only one prize hog he called Jigs. Jigs won seven blue ribbons over the years and many trophies. And he had his own pen all to himself. For Mr. Downing, saying good morning to Jigs each day just made him feel good all day long. Now the hog pen wasn't that far, just behind the barn a hundred and fifty feet away. Next to Jigs's pen was his mate Tilly's pen. Although she never won any blue ribbons, she was Jigs's girl, and the two were inseparable. As Mr. Downing turned the corner of the barn, there was Jigs, lying in the corner of his pen with his nose to the fence separating his pen from Tilly's snorting and whining.

"Why, Jigs? What are you doing stuffed in the corner like that? Are you looking for Tilly? She may be in the hog house, old boy. Let me go and look in there, boy."

Mr. Downing walked around the pen to look inside Tilly's hog house. As he got closer to the opening, he bent down on one knee to look inside, but Tilly wasn't in there. Mr. Downing got up and started looking around the pen for any openings in the fence to see if she wandered out. But there were no openings anywhere. He walked all around the rest of the property, trying to find Tilly. But she was nowhere to be found. Mr. Downing stood out in the middle of the road, scratching his head. Could it be that someone stole Tilly during the night? No! That couldn't be. They could not lift her over that fence without a hoist or something. And Jigs would have been squealing all through the night if anyone tried that. Mr. Downing started walking all around the ranch, calling out Tilly's name, hoping she would come out from some hidden corner or tree. But after an hour of looking, she was nowhere to be found.

Mrs. Downing came running out of the house onto the porch. She could hear her husband yelling and couldn't tell if he was hurt or something. She ran toward his voice and found him out by the property line huffing and puffing. "John, John, what's wrong? Are you all right?"

"Tilly's gone. She vanished right out of her pen. I've been looking all over the ranch for her, and there's no sign anywhere, like she up and flew away," said Mr. Downing.

Just then, he turned to his wife as if a bolt of lightning hit him. "Wait a minute. Flew away, flew away. That's it. I'm willing to bet Tilly did fly away in the claws of that giant eagle of Silas Livingston. Come on, dear, we are going into town to pay a visit to the sheriff's office. It's time we got rid of that beast from this town before everyone in the county has no more farm animals," said Mr. Downing, storming.

They both started back to the house, Mr. Downing flapping his arms, pointing to Tilly's pen, and Mrs. Downing trying to calm him down. Soon they reached the car, got in, and headed straight to town to see the sheriff.

As they pulled up into the parking spot by the sheriff, they were soon joined by Mr. and Mrs. Smith. Both got out of theirs and walked up the steps to the sheriff's office. Mr. Smith greeted Mr. Downing as they both were entering the office.

"Hello, John, you here to see the sheriff too?"

"I sure am. Tilly vanished from her pen last night, and I have an idea what happened to her. What are you here for?"

"One of my prize cows is missing also. Two big animals like ours, you'd think they had wings," replied Mr. Smith.

The two men just looked at each other and said, at the same time, "that eagle" and entered the sheriff's office.

Soon word spread throughout the whole town. People were afraid to leave their children outside alone, fearing they would be carried off. Suspicions of the eagle went from house to house like wild fire of how the giant eagle was carrying away cattle and all kinds of farm animals. The whole town was getting in an uproar. There was talk of capturing the eagle and destroying it. Others wanted to send for professional zoo people to come and catch the eagle and send him to a zoo somewhere far off out of the state. It was like "war of the worlds" all over again. The whole town was living in fear and all in a matter of only a few hours.

It was midafternoon at the Livingston farm. Mrs. Livingston was in the house making beds and cleaning. Silas was out by the horses, putting oats in their feed bags. And Solomon was up in his loft, resting. But this serene setting was soon shattered by the sound of Betty Jo yelling as she ran up the road toward the house, holding a newspaper in her hand.

"Silas, Silas, Mrs. Livingston, come quickly."

Mrs. Livingston came running out of the house, wiping her hands with a towel. Silas came running from behind the barn as they all met by the front porch.

"Betty Jo, what's wrong? Is everything all right home?" said Mrs. Livingston.

"Did you see this morning's paper? It's all about Solomon. Mr. Smith is missing his prize cow, and Tilly is missing from the Downing ranch. Everyone thinks that Solomon is responsible."

"But that's crazy. Solomon would never do anything like that. He's been in the barn all night," replied Silas.

"I know that, and you know that, but all those people in town are in an uproar right now, Silas, and they are out for blood— Solomon's blood," said Betty Jo.

"Mom, they'll come and try to take Solomon. They will kill him. We have to get him away from here and hide him somewhere. I won't let them harm him," said Silas.

Mrs. Livingston grabbed hold of Silas and held him close. "Don't you worry, no one is going to take Solomon anywhere. But we have to keep calm and think about this. First of all, we have to get Solomon somewhere safe where no one will think of looking until we can prove he didn't do all the things they said. Think, Silas, you know every inch of these mountains and forest. Is there any place big enough for Solomon where he will stay put?"

Then Silas thought of one place on the other side of Eagle Mountain, a cave that was thirty feet high and went back into the mountain about two hundred feet. There was an underground river that ran through the cave with fish, so Solomon would have food. And there were old timbers brought in by the old miners lying about that Solomon could use as a perch.

"It's perfect, Mom. Nobody ever goes near that place," said Silas.

"But will Solomon stay there and not come out?" asked Betty Jo.

"He will if I tell him to," answered Silas.

"But how will we get Solomon to the cave, Silas? You can't fly on him again, and the path getting there is narrow. We'll have to hike part of the way around the mountain. Solomon will have to follow us from the air," said Betty Jo.

Silas turned and looked at his mother. "Mom!"

Mrs. Livingston could only give in and agree. It was really the only way to protect Solomon at this point.

"All right, dear, go ahead, but please be careful and try to get back as soon as possible. There is much to be done. We have to find out whom or what took Tilly and Mr. Smith's cow."

"Thanks, Mom. Let's go, Betty Jo."

Silas and Betty Jo went out to the barn where Solomon sat perched up high in the loft. They climbed up to be face to beak with their friend.

"Listen to me, Solomon, you're in danger. A lot of people are blaming you for something you didn't do. So Betty Jo and I are going to take you to a place to hide out until we can clear this mess up. You're going to have to follow us to Eagle Mountain. There is an old cave where you can stay and be safe. There are fish there to eat, and I will come to see you when I can. You're going to have to trust me, old friend. Okay?"

Solomon gave a few small chirps and a nod of his head to signify he would follow.

Mrs. Livingston stood on the front porch, watching the road for any cars coming to pay a visit. Then, turning toward the barn, she saw Silas and Betty Jo riding off like the wind toward Eagle Mountain with Solomon flying just above them right on their heels. She watched until they were out of sight. Then, looking to heaven, she prayed, "Lord, please protect them out there in that dangerous county. Put your angels around Silas, Betty Jo, and Solomon and help us to solve this mystery. Thank you, Lord. Amen."

Meanwhile, the town meeting hall was filling up with people from all parts of the county. The news was spreading fast about the giant eagle that was carrying off farm animals of all shapes and sizes. Chairs were filling up as tempers grew high, and patients got low about what to do. Mr. Downing was telling people about the disappearance of Tilly over in one corner while Mr. Smith told his story about his missing prize cow right out of the pasture. Just then, the sheriff stepped up to the podium and asked everyone to be seated and to quiet down. Everyone took their seats, and the sheriff then began to speak.

"There have been some strange things happening in this town lately. I know. And I know many of you are concerned about the safety of your families and animals. Mr. Downing had a hog taken from him, and Mr. Smith over there had a prize cow taken. But thus far, no other animals have been taken. So we need to concern ourselves with these two cases. Now I know the story going around town about Solomon, Silas Livingston's eagle being the cause of all these. Now in case all of you have forgotten about the incident at the town picnic, you all were there and saw that bird save Silas from certain death, didn't you? And you also heard the account at the Livingston farm about Mrs. Livingston almost being devoured by wild dogs. So all I'm saying to you is, before we go pointing fingers in any direction, my men and I are going look into whom or what is the cause of these things. You all know the Livingstons as long as I have. You all knew Jim Livingston as a good, upstanding man in this town. To me, he was a good friend too until the Lord took him home."

Just then, Mr. Downing stood up to speak, saying, "Sure, Bob, we were all at the picnic and saw what that bird did. And we all heard about the incident at Livingston farm with the wild dogs. And we all know the Livingston family. Yes, they are good people, and we all like them a lot. All I'm saying to you and everyone here is I don't know of any creature that is able to pick up a cow or a hog and carry it off without at least leaving any blood marks or even destroying the hog fence. Who or whatever took Tilly and Mr. Smith's cow had tremendous strength, and I'm sorry, but the only creature that I can think off so far is that eagle. Believe me, I wouldn't do anything to harm the Livingstons. I'm just concerned about the safety of these people."

"As am I, Mr. Downing. As am I. I will be going out to the Livingston farm right after this meeting to talk to Silas. I may as well start my investigation there. I can assure all of you that I will get to the bottom of this and, if possible, get your animals back to you," replied the sheriff.

Mr. Smith got up and shouted, "I still think that bird is a danger to this town. We should go to the Livingston place and make that kid tell us where that eagle took our animals."

"I feel your pain, Mr. Smith, but you can't just go there like some lynch mob. This is not the Old West when people took the law into their own hands. And I can assure you, Mr. Smith, it's not going to happen here. Do I make myself clear? That goes for everyone else here. I'll go and talk to Silas and his mother. You folks go home and let the law take care of this. Everyone, go home now," replied the sheriff.

All the people started to leave the townhall, some satisfied, some not so satisfied. The sheriff turned to his deputy Charlie Potts.

"Charlie, get my car. We're going for a ride to the Livingston farm. And, Charlie, you better bring the shotgun just in case. Don't show it but keep it ready."

"Yes, sir, right away," replied Charlie.

Soon Silas and Betty Jo arrived at the cave on the other side of Eagle Mountain. Solomon was not far behind, landing on a felled tree next to the entrance of the cave. It was a huge opening carved out by time. They started in climbing over rocks and trees into the interior toward the back part of the cave, stepping over stones lying in the small river that ran through the center of the cave. The high ceiling would give Solomon room to fly around. They soon reached the back of the cave. Solomon perched himself on a timber, spread his giant wings, and gave a loud screech that echoed through the entire cave. Silas and Betty Jo ran up to him and threw their arms around his great neck.

"I love you, Solomon. And I will protect you. No one is going to ever take you away from me. Ever. But listen to me, old friend. You're going to have to stay here for a little while while Betty Jo and I figure out what happened to those animals. I will come back to check on you as soon as I can. You will safe in here until then."

The giant bird just looked at Silas, not knowing anything. To him, this was just another outing, and it was just as well. If Solomon suspected any harm to Silas or Betty Jo or his mother, the bird would react in the only way he knew how: to protect them. And that would be disastrous. Silas knew this from reading all about eagles and their habits. Silas was now protecting Solomon, but he was also protecting the townspeople should they take matters onto their own hands. Silas knew Solomon would fight back. Many people would be hurt or worse, and Solomon would most likely be shot.

"Come on, Betty Jo, we have to get back to the farm. I don't want to leave Mom there alone to face those people," said Silas.

"You're right, Silas. Do you think Solomon will be okay here by himself?" replied Betty Jo.

"He'll have to be for now."

As they started walking to the entrance of the cave, Silas looked back at Solomon. "Goodbye, Solomon. Stay here and wait for me, old friend. I'll be back. I promise."

Silas and Betty Jo exited the cave and headed back to their bikes where they left them on the path. Once they reached the bikes, they rode like the wind to get back to the farm, leaving a trail of dust behind them. As they got closer to the farm, Silas could see a car coming up the road toward the farm. They stopped their bikes on a small hill and watched as the car got closer and closer to the farm. Betty Jo turned to Silas.

"That's the sheriff's car, Silas. Looks like it's started. We had better get down there."

They put their feet to the pedals and rode as fast as they could down the narrow path toward the farm.

*****

There was a knock at the front door. Mrs. Livingston came into the kitchen and, looking out the window, saw the sheriff and his deputy standing there. She opened the door and stepped out to greet them.

"Why, hello, Bob, Charlie. What brings you here?"

"Hello, Sara, it's been a while, I know. How have you and been? Well, I hope," replied the sheriff.

"We're managing very well, thank you. And yes, it has been a while."

The sheriff looked to the ground a little embarrassed, then stood firmly and replied, "Well, I think you know why we're here. I guess you've heard all the talk going around town about the missing animals."

"Yes, Bob, I have heard all the stories going around about our giant eagle went and plucked up their prize cow and hog and flew off into the sunset for a Thanksgiving dinner. But I can tell you right now. Solomon did not do what everyone says he did. He was here the whole time, Bob. He could never hurt anything. It's just the way Silas trained him. You saw the way the children walked past him at the church. They all came within a few feet of him as he sat on that swing set, and one child was afraid."

"Yes, Sara, I was there. I saw. Silas has truly done an amazing job handling that bird, I know. But you have to understand that I still have to do my job. And until I find out what's going on, I still have to ask questions," replied the sheriff.

"Fine then, ask your questions."

Just then, Silas and Betty Jo came in from the back door and into the kitchen and stood next to his mother.

"Hello, Sheriff. Hello, Charlie," said Silas.

"Hello, Silas, Betty Jo, well then, I'm glad you're all here. I need to know where Solomon was last night, Silas," asked the sheriff.

"The town thinks that it's Solomon that took those animals, don't they, Sheriff? Well, Solomon would never do anything like that. He was up in his loft the whole time," answered Silas.

"And you know that for sure, son? Solomon wouldn't come out of the barn at night for anything?" asked Charlie.

"No, sir, eagles don't hunt at night. They hunt during the day. And anyway, Solomon only eats fish and leftovers that I give him. Sometimes, he will fly over to the river and bring back a nice salmon to his loft," said Silas.

"Where is the eagle now, Silas? Can we go to the barn and see him?" asked the sheriff.

The sheriff looked at all their faces when he asked that question. They all kind of looked off into the distance. Then he looked at Mrs. Livingston to get a straight answer.

"Sara, where is the bird?"

"He is not here, Bob. He is somewhere no one will harm him until we find out whom or what took those animals. Silas and Betty Jo are willing to help you in your investigation. They know these mountains and forest like nobody else. They can be of use to you, if you'll let them," replied Mrs. Livingston with a stern look on her face.

The sheriff knew he wouldn't find Solomon, so it wasn't worth looking. He was not on the farm. Then, looking at Charlie, then Betty Jo, then Silas, he finally just shook his head, smiled, and said, "I can't think of any two detectives that I would want on this case than the two of you. Get in the car, we have work to do."

Silas and Betty Jo ran to the sheriff's car and hopped in the back seat. The sheriff looked at Mrs. Livingston and gave her a little smile.

She, in return, smiled back and gestured with her lips, "Thank you, Bob."

"Sure thing, Sara," he said as he turned, put on his hat, and got into the car.

Off they drove down the road. She watched as the car disappeared around the corner, then she cast her eyes at Eagle Mountain where Solomon would have to hide out until this mystery was solved. She said in a low tone, "Stay there, Solomon. I pray you stay put for Silas's sake."

Charlie looked out the window of the car, staring at Eagle Mountain. It was a good distance away, and he wondered where Silas could have hidden a bird that size. Not many people ventured out to the mountain mainly because of the many small ledges and cliffs surrounding the mountain. Only those who knew the area well ever went there. And Charlie and the sheriff knew that Silas knew his way around those parts. Just then, Silas leaned forward and asked the sheriff, "Sheriff, why did Mr. Downing and Mr. Smith think Solomon had anything to do with the disappearance of the animals?"

"Well, son, there were no signs of any other animal tracks around the hog pen, and at Mr. Smith's pasture, the only tracks found out there were dear, fox, and rabbit. Even if there were mountain lion, we would have some blood tracks. But there was nothing at all, as if a five-hundred-pound cow just got lifted off the ground. You can't blame them, Silas, for thinking the way they do about your eagle. Right now, that's all we have until some other evidence turns up," replied the sheriff.

"Sheriff, I think we should go to the Downing ranch. If Solomon was anywhere near that hog pen, Silas would know. He would have left signs of something there. Do you think Mr. Downing would let us take a look around?" asked Betty Jo.

"Well, it can't hurt to try, and it can only help. Let's give it a shot," replied the sheriff.

There was about an hour left of daylight. Mr. and Mrs. Downing sat on the front porch, pondering all that had happened. The sky was turning bright red and orange off in the western horizon. Mrs.

Downing noticed a small cloud of dust approaching down the road. She stood up and saw that it was the sheriff's car.

"Dear, it's Bob coming to pay us a visit. Looks like some other people are in the car with him."

As the car drove up to the house, Mrs. Downing could see Betty Jo and Silas in the back seat.

"Why, it's Silas and Betty Jo with the sheriff."

Mr. Downing got up and went to the car as the sheriff got out; they met halfway. The sheriff shook Mr. Downing's hand as they talked while Silas and Betty Jo remained in the car.

"Mr. Downing, I took a ride out to the Livingston farm and had a talk with Silas and his mother and Betty Jo. Silas believes his bird had nothing to do with the disappearance of Tilly or Mr. Smith's cow. But he and Betty Jo are willing to help us find out what did happen to those animals if you will let them. If anyone knows that bird, it's Silas. Is it okay if we look around Tilly's pen?" asked the sheriff.

"Well, I guess it would be all right. But I already looked all around there. I couldn't find anything," said Mr. Downing.

"Can't hurt to look again," replied the sheriff.

The sheriff waved for Charlie, Betty Jo, and Silas to get out of the car. They all headed down to Tilly's pen to look around. Silas walked next to Mr. Downing.

"I'm very sorry, Mr. Downing, about Tilly. I hope I can help to find out what happened to her. I hope you won't hold it against my mom for anything that I may have done," said Silas.

"Believe me, son, I've known your family for years. I knew your dad when he was a boy. It's not very often a town gets to see a giant eagle flying all over their town with a boy riding on its back. But if you can prove that something other than your eagle took Tilly, I'll be the first to admit I was wrong," replied Mr. Downing.

The sheriff and Betty Jo could hear the conversation as they walked in front. They both felt a little relief that Mr. Downing did not hold Silas personally responsible for Tilly's disappearance.

There was about a half hour of light left as they all arrived at Tilly's pen. Nothing looked disturbed. No other animal tracks. No broken fence. They all spread out and looked around the whole area. Silas and Jo wandered over the far north corner of the pen and scanned the whole area. Nothing seemed to catch their eye that was not normal until Silas noticed something sticking out between the fence and a board. He waited until no one was looking, then reached down quickly and put it in his jacket. It was now too dark to see much of anything.

"We had better get going back, Silas, Betty Jo. Your parents will be worried. There is nothing here," said the sheriff.

They all headed back to the car. Before climbing in, Silas turned to Mr. Downing and said, "Thank you for letting us look around, sir."

"You're welcome, son. I hope we find the answers we're looking for," replied Mr. Downing.

They all got into the car and headed for home. Silas was quiet all the way home, and as the car pulled up to Silas's front door, he and Betty Jo got out, saying to the sheriff, "Thanks for letting us tag along, Sheriff."

"You kids just be sure to let me know if you find anything. And, Silas, keep that bird out of sight and no joyrides. Understand!" replied the sheriff.

Just then, Mrs. Livingston came on to the front porch.

"Silas, dinner is ready. Betty Jo, I'll drive you home after dinner. Bob, would you and Charlie like to join us for dinner?"

"Thanks, Sara, but Charlie and I have to get back to town. I'll have to take a rain check," replied Bob.

Mrs. Livingston waved goodbye as Silas and Betty Jo flew by into the kitchen and over to the sink to wash their hands. Silas watched from the kitchen window as the sheriff drove off down the road. His mother was still on the porch. Silas pulled Betty Jo out of sight from the window to show her what he picked up at the Downing place.

"Betty Jo, look what I found by Tilly's pen."

Silas opened his jacket and pulled out an eagle's feather. Betty Jo's eyes widened. It could have been any eagle's feather. But it only made the evidence against Solomon worse. Just then, Mrs. Livingston came in, and Silas tucked the feather away.

After dinner, Mrs. Livingston drove Betty Jo home, and Silas went to his room to get ready for bed. Taking the feather from his jacket, he sat on the bed, running his hand over the feather and looking out the window at Eagle Mountain where Solomon stayed hidden in the cave. His mind wandered back and forth, wondering if Solomon could do what everyone said he did. Soon he could hear his mother drive up to the house and enter the kitchen. The footsteps got closer to the door as his mom entered the room and sat down. Silas was still holding the eagle's feather in his hand and looking at his mother.

"Betty Jo told me about the feather you found at the Downing place. It doesn't prove anything, Silas. Solomon was here the whole time up in that barn. That feather could belong to any number of eagle's flying around the area."

"I know, Mom. It just doesn't make things better either. We have to find out what happened to Tilly and Mr. Smith's cow because right now, everything points to Solomon," replied Silas.

"Try to get some sleep, son." Mrs. Livingston kissed Silas on the forehead and walked slowly out of the room and closed the door.

Silas then prayed, "Lord, only you know if Solomon did or didn't do these things. I pray you reveal the truth, Lord, and give me the courage to accept it and deal with it. Amen."

The next morning, while Mrs. Livingston was preparing breakfast, she could hear Silas mulling around in his room, digging through his closet. When he finally came out, he had his backpack as if he were going on a hike somewhere.

"What's with the backpack, Silas? Going somewhere?" asked Mrs. Livingston.

"I have to check on Solomon, Mom. Then I'd be heading over to the Downing place again. I may find something else besides this feather that will help solve this puzzle," replied Silas.

"Well, not until you have done your morning chores, young man. And after you have checked on Solomon, come home and I will go to the Downing ranch with you," said Mrs. Livingston.

"Yes, Mom." And out he went to do his chores, taking an apple from the counter as he went out the door.

Solomon remained back at the cave, just as Silas had told him. There were plenty of fish on hand in the small river, but Solomon was beginning to get fidgety and wanted to get out to spread his wings. It wasn't easy being cooped up. As long as Silas kept coming to visit, it gave Solomon the patience to stay put. Silas didn't know how long before Solomon got tired and left the cave. So he had to come by every day to visit the bird. It was a long trek every day, but he had to keep Solomon out of sight until they got some answers. And hopefully, those answers would come soon. Finding that feather at the Downing ranch was really beginning to worry Silas. All kinds of things were going through his head. He didn't know what he would do if Solomon were to be taken from him and put in some far-off zoo or, worse, destroyed. He raced through his chores and ran back to the house, flying through the kitchen door.

"Done with my chores, Mom. Can we go now?"

"That was fast. Sure everything got done?" replied his mom.

"Yes, Mom."

"Okay then, let me get my car keys, and we'll go collect Betty Jo and head over to the Downing ranch. You go get cleaned up."

Soon they were driving down the road toward the Downing ranch. Silas was looking out the passenger window at Eagle Mountain. There was a dark gray cloud hanging just below the mountain peak, and he could see just the point sticking up above the cloud. It was a strange sight. Then, in a split second, he noticed something flying out of the cloud and back in again in the blink of an eye. Rubbing his eyes and straining to see if it happened again, he stared for a while, but whatever it was didn't come back out. Betty Jo and Mrs. Livingston were focused on the road ahead. Silas didn't say anything but kept his eyes on the mountain as they drove on further away from Eagle Mountain.

As they drove up the road to the Downing ranch, they noticed that the sheriff was already there talking to the Downings. There were also some other people alongside the sheriff speaking to the Downings.

As they pulled up closer, Silas rolled down the window; he could hear the sheriff saying to the other people, "Here are the Livingstons now." Then they all started walking over to the car.

As they all exited the car, the sheriff said, "Sara, Silas, Betty Jo, these people are from *N ational Geographic*. They heard about Solomon and would like to do a story on him. This is Peter Fielding, a writer for the magazine, and this is Jerry Palmer, a photographer also for the magazine."

Both men shook hands with Silas and Mrs. Livingston and Betty Jo.

"Hello, Silas. It's not everyday people hear about a boy who flies on a giant eagle. Our magazine is worldwide, son, and just think of the publicity this small town would get. There would be people from all over the world coming here to see and write about Solomon," said Mr. Fielding.

"Yes, indeed, and the income all the stores and hotels around here would benefit from, it would put this town on the map," said Mr. Palmer.

It was then that the sheriff and Mrs. Livingston, looking at each other, realized that this was not what they really wanted. Being put on the map was one thing. Being overrun with thousands of people so suddenly would destroy their peaceful community. Silas and Betty Jo looked at each other and thought the same thing. Solomon would no longer belong to them but to the world. It would be a freak show. And that was one thing Silas was not about to let happen.

"No, they'll just stick him in a zoo somewhere so people can come and gawk at him. He can't be in a cage. He'll just die there. He needs his freedom. Eagles have to fly. They own the sky. It's their kingdom," yelled Silas.

"Silas is right, Mrs. Livingston. Solomon would only die in a cage," said Betty Jo.

The two men from the magazine looked at each other.

"The kids have a point, Peter," said Mr. Palmer. "We've been doing wildlife stories for a long time. A bird that size would never survive captivity."

"So what do we do? The magazine knows about Solomon. They want a story, and that's what we were sent here to get. I'm with you and the kids here. I love animals too. So how do we do this?" said Mr. Fielding.

"First things first, everyone. We still have an issue of some missing animals, remember!" said the sheriff.

"Perhaps if we all put our heads together and try to solve this mystery, we can all relax and get on with our lives," replied Mrs. Livingston.

"Good idea, Sara. Let's go over this place with a fine-tooth comb, and maybe we'll find out what really happened to those animals," said the sheriff.

As they all walked to where Tilly was last seen, Mrs. Livingston stayed back a bit from Silas, Betty Jo, and the sheriff. Walking beside the two men from the magazine, she said to them in private, "I know that you came here to do a story and that you really can't go back empty-handed to your higher ups. Promise me that you won't write anything until we find out what happened here. If you are going to write anything, it should be the truth. Promise me."

They both shook their heads in agreement.

"This is going to be a tough one, Jerry, but she's right. If I'm going to print anything, I want it to be the truth."

They both shook hands in silence.

"Okay, let's do some real investigative reporting," said Peter.

Soon they neared the spot where the hog disappeared.

"Let's separate and see if we can find anything. I don't care how small it is. Whatever we find, bring it to me, and we'll check it out," said the sheriff.

Suddenly, Silas remembered the feather he found the last time they were there. Reaching into his pocket, Silas pulled out the feather.

"What is that, Silas?" asked the sheriff.

"It's a feather I found the last time we were here," replied Silas.

"You've had that feather all this time, Silas?" asked the sheriff.

They all gathered around the feather, wondering.

"Hey! I know a guy back at the magazine who does research on stuff like this. He can get DNA test to see what and where this feather came from," said Mr. Palmer.

They all looked at one another.

"Well, we don't have anything to lose at this stage of the game," said Mrs. Livingston.

"Well, okay, then, but be careful with that. It's all we have," said Silas.

"Don't worry, son. This guy is the best at what he does. Believe me, he'll find out who owns this feather. If we leave now, we can get back here in a few days," said Mr. Fielding.

They all agreed, and the two men hopped back in their car and headed back to the city to catch a plane back to the magazine office. Then they all resumed their search for more answers to this mystery.

Meanwhile, back in town, the people were having a meeting of their own in the townhall. There was a lot of talk about getting a mob together and going out hunting for Solomon and shooting him. Standing in the back of the hall was Charlie, listening to all the complaints and grumbling.

"This sounds like a lynch mob if ever I heard one. I'd better get hold of the sheriff and tell him what's going on here," he said in a low voice so no one could hear. And out the door he ran, jumping into the squad car and racing off to the Downing ranch.

One of the ladies at the hall was looking out the window and noticed Charlie speeding off. "Looks like Charlie is in a hurry to get somewhere," she said to a man standing next to her.

He peered out the window to see a cloud of smoke speeding down the main drag of town. "Looks like he's headed for the Downing ranch. I believe the sheriff is there today with the Livingston kid and his mom." Then the man turned to the crowd and yelled out, "Hey, everyone, Charlie is headed to the Downing place to tell the sheriff about what we were all talking about here. Once the sheriff finds out, he'll try to stop it. We better get moving and get that bird quick before he grabs one of our kids next."

They all started exiting the hall in a hurry.

One person yelled out, "All you men get your guns. We'll meet out at the base of Eagle Mountain, then we'll form into parties of five and spread out. With any luck, we'll have that bird plucked and gutted by sundown."

With that, they all jumped into their vehicles and headed home to arm themselves to get ready for the hunt for Solomon.

Meanwhile, back at the Downing ranch, the sheriff and his little group of detectives were busy looking for more clues to clear Solomon. Silas and Betty Jo were busy looking in Tilly's pen while the sheriff and Mrs. Livingston wandered out into the field next to the pen to search for anything that looked out of place.

"How could a seven-hundred-pound hog just disappear, Bob? It's as if she was plucked up and carried off," said Mrs. Livingston.

"That's just it, Sara. Plucked up. Even Solomon with his size, I don't see how even he could have picked up Tilly and carried her off so easily," replied the sheriff.

In the distance, they could hear the sound of a car racing up the road. Turning to see who it was, the sheriff said, "Why, it's Charlie, and he's moving pretty fast. Let's go see what's up."

They all hurried to meet Charlie as he jumped out of the car. "Hurry, Sheriff, it's the townspeople. They are all heading to Eagle Mountain to hunt down that eagle and shoot it." Charlie just looked at Silas.

"Sheriff, you have to stop them. Solomon belongs to me. They have no right to just shoot him. They still don't know if he even did it. Besides, if Solomon thinks he's in danger, he will attack, and someone will get hurt for sure."

"The boy's right. My pa had a nest of eagles on the mountain by our farm in Arizona, and if you got close to them, they would just swoop down on ya. I guess they thought you might be trying to get to the babies," said Charlie.

"We need to go right now. Everyone, in the cars," ordered the sheriff.

They all jumped in the cars and headed for Eagle Mountain.

At the base of the mountain, men started gathering. Each had a rifle and sidearm. They had water canteens, backpacks, and food. It looked like they were going back to war. A big man climbed up on a rock and waved to the men.

"Okay, let's all break up into groups of five. Each group go in a different direction, and whoever meets up with that bird first, fire a shot in the air. Got it?" said the leader of the group. This man looked tough. A veteran of World War II, battle-hardened with scars on his neck, he had gotten from fighting a German in the trenches alongside hundreds of other soldiers. His name was John Steel, fitting for a man of his stature. After losing his wife to cancer three years ago and running a hardware store alone, he lost his humor, always talking about the war and friends he lost. Now he had a mission: hunt down this bird like the enemy and kill it. He felt like he had some purpose after being cooped up in that store with nuts and bolts and tools. John jumped down off the rock. "Okay, let's head out."

They all went in different directions. This was no war assignment; this was a mob.

"Can we go any faster?" asked Silas, sitting in the back seat.

"We're almost there, son, just a few more miles. There's Eagle Mountain now."

Silas and Betty Jo leaned forward, looking out the front window.

As they got closer to the road leading to the base of the mountain, Charlie noticed all the cars parked. "Looks like they already started their hunt, Sheriff," said Charlie.

Pulling up to the cars, they noticed some women standing by the cars, waiting. The sheriff walked over and, speaking firmly, asked, "Where did they go, ladies?"

They all just looked at him with a numb stare.

"Look, I know your husbands and boyfriends know how to hunt deer and elk and rabbits and such, but we're not talking about just any normal animal here. Plus, many of those men don't know Eagle Mountain, its many winding trails and hills. People have gotten lost out there. And if eagles know they are being hunted, they will defend their territory. Believe me, someone is going to get hurt."

Now the women started thinking twice about keeping silent. Just then, one of the women spoke up. "They all went in different directions in groups of five."

The other women tried to stop her, but she told them. "I'm not going to lose my husband over some bird hunt. He's just following because all the other men are following that John Steel. He doesn't want them to think he's afraid. We still don't know if Silas's eagle did it anyway. What if they are all out there on some wild goose chase and someone gets hurt or killed looking for this bird? Is it worth it?"

The sheriff then turned to Charlie. "You go and get some of the other deputies from the next town and tell them to meet me here. We are going to find this bunch and stop this right now."

Charlie jumped in his car and road off.

"Sara, you better stay with me here. Silas, you and Betty Jo better go to wherever you hid Solomon and make sure he doesn't show his beak or they will shoot him for sure. Understand?" said the sheriff sternly.

The sheriff just looked at Mrs. Livingston. "This is maddening," he said, running his hands through his hair.

Meanwhile, Charlie pulled up to the sheriff's office to grab a few things before heading over to the next town. As he ran into the building, the phone began ringing. Charlie picked it up, clamoring to grab something out of the desk.

"Hello, sheriff's office, Charlie speaking."

It was Mr. Palmer from *National Geographic* magazine. He and Mr. Fielding returned to get info on the feather that Silas had found at the Downing ranch. And their information made Charlie stop in his tracks.

"Are you sure? Oh my gosh, I need to tell the sheriff before they go wandering out there. Thank you, Mr. Palmer. I'll tell the sheriff." Charlie hung up the phone and stood there dumbfounded. "Holy cow," he said to himself. Then he remembered what the sheriff said about going to get more men to help. He raced out the door and, jumping in the car, raced off to get help from the next town. He knew they had a lot more men there. It was a bigger town. Charlie knew most of the deputies there. They had all gone to school together, and everyone knew one another in some way or another. The town was only eight miles away, and Charlie flew down the road, leaving a cloud of dust in his path.

Silas and Betty Jo arrived at the cave where Solomon was waiting patiently. Climbing over felled trees and rocks, they entered the cave to see Solomon perched on his tree limb, dead fish all around him. Seeing Silas and Betty Jo, he gave out a loud screech. He was happy to see them. Silas and Betty Jo wrapped their arms around his great neck.

"Looks like you're going to have to stay here a little while longer, Solomon. There are men out there trying to hurt you. They think you took Mr. Downing's prize hog. You're going to have to stay put here. Nobody really knows about this place but me and Betty Jo. So you will be safe here. I see you found enough fish to eat."

Betty Jo looked at Silas. "You know, eventually, they will find this place if they are persistent, especially with that John Steel fella leading them. I hope the sheriff can stop them before this gets really out of hand," said Betty Jo.

"Me too. The sheriff has a way of talking to people. I hope so too," replied Silas.

They both sat by Solomon, rubbing his neck and keeping him company so that he stayed calm and remained in the cave.

Charlie reached the sheriff's office and, racing inside, told the chief there about the mob. They had all heard about Solomon and didn't think he was a threat. But they knew what could happen when a mob got together and out of hand.

"Jim, you get about ten men together and go with Charlie here to go help Bob with this. He is going to need help on this one," said the chief.

"You bet, sir. Let's go, guys."

Jim and ten men all grabbed rifles from the gun cabinet and radios, and all jumped into three cars and followed Charlie to Eagle Mountain.

Meanwhile, the sheriff and Mrs. Livingston stayed at the base of the mountain with the other women, waiting for Charlie to return with help.

"There isn't much we can do until Charlie and the deputies get here, Sara. We have to get those men back here before one of them gets hurt. That mountain has always been a strange place. Lots of secret, hidden paths. My dad told me stories. That's why I have always kept my distance from this mountain," said the sheriff.

Mrs. Livingston could only think of how many times Silas went to that mountain. But he always came back. She felt someone or something was protecting him, as if he was the only one aloud to be there.

In the distance, a sound of cars getting nearer could be heard.

"That must be Charlie and the deputies."

They were making a cloud of dust as they drove down the dirt road to the base of the mountain where the sheriff and Mrs. Livingston waited.

"Hi, Jim, boys, glad you could come and help," said the sheriff.

"No problem, Bob. What do we have here?"

"We have about twenty men scattered up in this mountain, trying to hunt down Solomon, the Livingston boy's eagle. I guess you all heard the story."

"Yes, we did. Saw all the news about him on TV. So what do these men think this bird did anyway?" asked Jim.

"Well, we have a prize hog and a cow missing," replied the sheriff.

"I see, and they believe this eagle is responsible. Okay! Let's go bring them back. What's your plan, Bob?"

"I guess we better all split up since that's what they did and try to find each party. We'll split up in groups of three and try to cover as much ground as possible."

"Sounds good, let's go, men," said Jim.

They all split and went off down different trails.

"Don't worry, Sara, we'll find them. Go back home and wait. You just make sure Silas keeps that bird out of sight."

"I will. You just be careful up there." She then kissed him on the cheek with a look of concern.

"You bet," he replied as he smiled and walked off with Charlie.

Charlie just turned and smiled in approval.

She watched as they got further and further away, then disappeared around a turn, going deeper into the mountain.

"Oh, by the way, Sheriff, I forgot to tell you. You got a call from those magazine people that were here. That fella they knew did some research on that feather that Silas found at the Downing ranch. It's not an eagles feather at all."

The sheriff turned to Charlie. "What is it?" he asked.

"It's a condor feather," Charlie replied.

"A condor. My gosh, Charlie, a normal-sized condor is what? Twenty to twenty-five pounds. And a normal-sized eagle is probably seven to fourteen pounds. My god. That means that thing could be twice the size of Solomon. And those men are walking right into its path. We need to warn Jim and the others." The sheriff grabbed his radio. "Jim, Jim, do you read me?"

"Jim here, Sheriff. What's up?"

"Jim, I just found out. We are dealing with two giant birds here, not one. There is a giant condor up there, and those men are headed straight for it. We have to move fast and find them before it finds them."

"Holy cow, a condor. That thing is going to be massive. You got it, Bob. I'll alert the others."

The sheriff looked at Charlie. "That makes sense now. Solomon could never pick up a hog, but a giant condor, that's it. Come on, Charlie, we need to move it."

*****

In the cave sat three quiet figures. The sound were only of the water rippling past them and the small birds flying in and out, stopping on a branch, chirping away. All they could do was wait; it was nerve-racking not knowing what was going on beyond the cave.

"The sheriff will find those men and put a stop to this nonsense, Silas. I'm sure of it," said Betty Jo.

"I sure hope so. Don't worry, Solomon, the sheriff will find those men. No one is going to shoot you."

"We need to get back and check on your mom, Silas. She's all alone, wondering what happened to us," said Betty Jo.

"Right, we need to go, boy. You're going to have to stay here a little while longer, my friend. We'll be back soon. Come on, Betty Jo."

They both said their goodbyes to Solomon and started for home.

As the sheriff and Charlie climbed the path, they could hear voices. Turning a corner, there was some of the men talking. The sheriff then said, "You men stay right where you are."

"It's the sheriff," one of them said.

"Okay, the party is over. You men get back down this mountain to your wives before you worry them sick."

"What about that bird, Sheriff? Is he just going to get off scot-free?"

"For your information, we just found out we are not dealing with just one giant bird here, Bill. There's a giant condor up there. It's a good thing you stopped to take a break or you all would be meeting it in person," replied Charlie.

Then one of them remembered. "Hey, John Steel went on ahead of us. He's up there alone."

"Oh no!" said the sheriff. "Charlie, you get these men down. I'll go up and try to find him."

"Right, Sheriff. Okay, boys, let's get going," Charlie replied.

One by one, they fell in line and started back down the trail. The sheriff watched as Charlie disappeared around the bend, then looked up at the mountain before him. "Well, here it goes. Okay, John Steel, where did you get to?" said the sheriff to himself out loud.

Taking a deep breath, he started up the steep trail. When he got to a ledge, he could see down to the base the cars parked and the women standing there, waiting. They looked tiny. Then he saw a group of people walking toward the car from the west. It was some of the other men the deputies found.

"Good job, Jim. I guess they didn't get too far. Now to find you, John Steel."

As the sheriff climbed higher, the trail got narrower and steeper. There were rocks in the path. One wrong move and its five hundred feet down. The sheriff wondered how Silas knew his way around this mountain. He climbed it many times. "Silas, you must be part mountain goat," he said aloud.

About a hundred feet further up the trail, John Steel climbed huffing and puffing. He was not in the same shape as he was when he was in the military. He stopped to sit on a rock and take a breath. Looking out over the whole area, he could see what Silas saw while riding atop Solomon. Then, gazing down the mountainside, he could also see all the men gathered around the cars. He knew now that the hunt was over for them and that the sheriff must now be involved. But he was determined to find Solomon. He gathered his strength and continued up the narrow path, kicking rocks and sometimes tripping and catching his balance. "That kid must be part mountain goat," he said as he tripped over another rock.

Back at the Livingston ranch, Silas and Betty Jo were just arriving home. Mrs. Livingston was waiting in the kitchen.

"Mom, we're back," said Silas as they both came in the door.

"Oh my gosh, Silas, Betty Jo. I was wondering when you would get back. How is Solomon?"

"He's fine, Mom. What's happening with the sheriff and all those men hunting for Solomon?"

"I don't know, son, but I think we should get back to where the sheriff started at the base of Eagle Mountain. Let's take the pickup. It's faster."

Silas and Betty Jo grabbed their bikes and put them in the back of the pickup. They all got into the vehicle and headed back to the mountain base. It wasn't far, and they reach the road entrance in a few minutes.

As they neared the area, they could see a crowd of people standing by their cars, staring up at the mountain. Charlie was sitting on the hood of his car, talking to one of the deputies. They all got out and ran over to where Charlie was sitting.

As they got closer, they heard the word *condor*. It seemed everybody around them was saying that word.

Mrs. Livingston walked up to Charlie, putting her hand on his shoulder. "Charlie, what are they all talking about? I keep hearing them mention condor," she asked.

With Silas and Betty Jo standing by, Charlie told them about what the men from the magazine said. The feather Silas found was a condor feather and that there could be a giant condor on the loose and that it was most likely responsible for the missing cow and hog. It was then that Silas remembered that he saw something flying above Eagle Mountain, then disappearing in the cloud.

"I think I saw it," said Silas.

"What? When was this?" replied Charlie.

"When we were heading over to the Downing ranch the day we met those magazine men. I was looking out the window of the car and caught something out the corner of my eye flying high in the cloud. Then it just disappeared. I didn't think anything of it at the time."

"Holy cow, the sheriff and John Steel are still up there. We managed to get the others down, but that Steel fella wanted to go on alone, and the sheriff went after him alone. If they cross paths with that condor, they are both dead men," said Charlie.

"Oh my, Charlie, what do we do? By now, they're both close to the top. We could never reach them in time," cried Mrs. Livingston. "That condor will be twice the size of Solomon. He could carry both of them away."

Silas to the Rescue

Now the sheriff was almost at the summit, which was a large plateau that was a hundred feet below the peak. Climbing a narrow path and turning a corner, he could hear moaning. He turned toward the sound and saw John Steel lying face down in a crevice. He had a large bolder on his right foot wedged in beneath some rocks. The sheriff hurried down to help, rushing to his side to lift the bolder. John Steel looked in surprise.

"Sheriff, didn't expect to see you."

"Looks like you got yourself into a real fix here, John Steel. But we need to get you out of here and back down this mountain fast. There's a giant condor loose living up here, and we don't want to become its next meal."

"You mean we have two giant birds flying around here?"

"Yes, and this baby is twice the size of Solomon. I'll try to lift this bolder. Soon as I get it high enough, you pull your leg out," said the sheriff.

The sheriff reached down under the bolder to get a good grip, then, turning to John Steel, said, "Ready, one, two, three, go." The sheriff lifted the bolder a few inches, and John Steel pulled his leg free. They both looked at each other in relief.

"Thanks, Sheriff," said John Steel as he took a deep breath.

As the sheriff grabbed hold of John Steel suddenly, a dark shadow covered them.

Looking down at them perched on a rock were two hungry eyes of that giant condor. As both men jerked back at the sight, the sheriff slipped backward, and his gun fell from its holster, falling off a ledge, causing it to fire a shot.

Everyone standing at the base of the mountain all looked up, hearing the shot.

One of the deputies said, "Something is wrong up there."

Then Silas came forward. "Mom, there's only one chance: Solomon. He can get me up there fast and get Mr. Steel and the sheriff down off the top of that mountain."

"No, Silas, it's too dangerous. You could get killed. No."

"Mom, it's the only way."

One of the deputies then said, "I can't see any other way, Mrs. Livingston. Your boy is the only one who knows how to ride that bird. He's already shown us that."

"Mom, we are wasting time. They could be hurt."

"All right, Silas, but be careful."

"Go get 'em, son," said Charlie.

The cave wasn't far. Silas grabbed his bike from the pickup.

Betty Jo ran over to him. "Silas, be careful."

"I will," he replied. Then Silas jumped on his bike and rode like the wind, flying through narrow gullies and path and over hills, and, in no time, was back in the cave, splashing through the water and yelling, "Solomon, I'm here, boy. We have a job to do, friend. The sheriff is in trouble and needs our help. We have to go to the top of Eagle Mountain. Are you up for another ride?"

Solomon gave out a loud screech and stretched out his huge wings. Silas climbed on his neck.

"Let's go, Solomon."

From out the mouth of the cave was a sight to be seen: a boy and his eagle, soaring like a jet and climbing high toward the top of Eagle Mountain. They ascended higher and higher.

The crevice that the sheriff and John Steel were trapped in was too narrow for the condor to reach them. The giant bird kept stretching its head in, trying to pull them out. Both men kicked at the giant beak and threw rocks to keep it at bay. The bird kept coming, pecking at them. All they could see was the inside of its mouth as it came closer and closer, digging at the ground and moving rocks, trying to get to the two men.

Then, when all seemed lost, the condor was suddenly pulled back by two giant talons grasping the condor's head and dragging backward. As the men climbed out the crevice, there before them was Solomon with his huge, outstretched wings and Silas on his neck, dragging the giant condor away. Both birds were screeching and flapping wildly.

The sheriff saw that Silas could be hurt in this battle. He yelled, "Silas, Silas, jump off. Get off quickly."

Silas waited for the right moment, then, when Solomon touched the ground during this bird fight, he slid off and rolled away to avoid getting caught between the birds. The sheriff ran over, and pulling Silas aside by John Steel, they watched as these two birds battled it out in the air, tearing into each other with their huge talons and giant beaks, spinning wildly in the air like a dog fight in wartime.

Then, as they separated and circled to attack, Solomon's eyes were fixed on the condor's throat, and with a sudden burst, Solomon descended, picking up speed, and then, extending his giant talons, caught the condor square in the neck and dug deep into its throat, then flew straight toward the edge of the mountain and drove the condor against a sharp rock. Solomon then let go of the condor, flew up, and just hovered above it until the condor tilted its head and died.

The sheriff, John Steel, and Silas stood back and watched as Solomon landed next to them, then gave out a loud screeching sound of victory. Silas ran over to his friend and threw his arms around him. "You did it, Solomon. You did it."

The sheriff and John Steel walked over to Silas and Solomon. "You sure did, son, both of you. You saved our lives, son," said the sheriff. The Sheriff looked at John Steel. "Well, John!"

John Steel went over to Silas and Solomon. "Silas, forgive me, son, for all the trouble I've caused to you and to Solomon here. I guess I'm just an old fool."

"It's okay, Mr. Steel. One thing we did find out. At least, we know now the mystery of what happened to Tilly and the cow," replied Silas.

Looking over at the dead condor, the sheriff said, "What you say we get down off this mountain?"

Silas climbed aboard Solomon and, looking at both men, said, "See you two at the base of Eagle Mountain." Then, with a sudden thrust, Solomon and the boy flew off.

"Okay, John, let's go home."

The two men started off down the mountain, taking one last look at the dead condor and realizing how close they both came to not ever getting out of there alive.

The scene a few hours later at the base of Eagle Mountain was a lot more cheerful. John Steel was being treated by medics for his injury to his foot. Many of the wives were hugging their husbands while scolding them for going off on a foolish quest. Charlie and the deputies were talking police talk over by their squad cars. Silas, Betty Jo, Mrs. Livingston, and the sheriff huddled around Solomon.

"So, Bob, when are you going to come over for dinner more often? Seems like you and Solomon should become closer friends," said Mrs. Livingston, smiling.

"I would like that," replied Bob.

"I would like that too," said Silas.

A few feet away, there came a voice no one knew. "You people seem to have had your work cut out for you these past few months."

They all turned to see a man, tall and lean.

He had on a gray suit and a fedora and was holding a pipe in his mouth. "Allow me to introduce myself. My name is Robert Oppenheimer, and judging from the size of your eagle friend there, I believe I am probably the cause of all these. I'm here because I read all about Solomon in the newspapers. He has become a real attraction. But after reading all the articles about this amazing boy here who actually tamed him, well, I just had to come and see for myself."

Silas walked over to Mr. Oppenheimer and held out his hand. "I know all about you, sir. You helped to win the war. But it wasn't just me. This is Betty Jo Stevens. She and my mom both helped to raise Solomon," said Silas.

"Well then, I commend you all. We all knew about the effects of radiation on animals, but I have never really witnessed it until now. Truly amazing," he replied.

The sheriff walked over to Mr. Oppenheimer and shook his hand. "Thank you, sir, for your amazing contribution in winning the war."

Then Mrs. Livingston stepped up. "Mr. Oppenheimer, would you like to join the sheriff and my family here for dinner? I'm sure Silas and Betty Jo and Bob have a million questions they would like to ask you."

"Thank you, Mrs. Livingston. I would be delighted."

"We'll meet you home, Mom. Come on, Betty Jo."

The two went over to Solomon, and climbing up on his neck, Silas cried out, "Up we go, Solomon."

On with his huge wings spread out, he lifted himself up, and off they went. The sheriff, Mrs. Livingston, and Mr. Oppenheimer looked as they flew off in the sunset. A beautiful sight in the sky.

"Boy, to be a kid again," said Mr. Oppenheimer.

"Meet you at the house, Bob. Mr. Oppenheimer, you can ride with me in the pickup. I also have some questions for you," said Mrs. Livingston.

They all climbed in the vehicles, and everyone started for home. This would be the talk of the town for years to come.

Meanwhile, back on the summit laid the dead condor. The sun was going down on the horizon, and not far from the dead bird was a nest, and within the nest, was one egg. Standing next to the condor, looking off at the town below and all the cars heading home, was the old Indian who met Silas on his first journey to the top of Eagle Mountain. The old Indian looked back at the egg, then turned toward the town again and gave a slight smile, then turned and walked off and disappeared around one of the many trails.

The End

ABOUT THE AUTHOR

Tom Puma is a retired electrician and real estate agent. He has been writing since 1980. His first book, *The Adventures of Tom and Fiore*, was published in 1982. His second book, *The Bully*, was released this spring of 2023.

Tom grew up on Staten Island, New York, living a life full of adventure like Tom Sawyer and Huckleberry Finn. He decided to write about these adventures and the memories of the childhood and teen years, which is where he gets much of his imagination from. Tom always believed in finding his true passion, which is writing, and tries to instill this concept in everyone he meets, finding that passion that lies deep within all of us.

Tom lives in Cave Creek, Arizona, where he enjoys his two and a half acres of solitude to work on his writing projects. When Tom is not writing, he enjoys studying history, Bible study, art shows, singing doo-wop, and listening to opera. Tom also supports Saint Jude Children's Research Hospital, where 25 percent of his royalties will go. "No child should have cancer. Every kid should be allowed to be a kid."